Innes Yates was born in Edinburgh. She has written short stories, poetry and novels since childhood.

After gaining a degree in Art and Design, she moved to London where she taught art for many years before retraining in Specific Learning Difficulties. This enabled her to teach children and adults in schools and colleges, helping them to achieve academic qualifications.

At weekends, Innes worked with the Police teaching young offenders and, in the evenings, sang in her husband's rock band at different venues around North London.

She now lives on the East coast of Scotland.

Innes Yates

# THE YELLOW FIELD

AUSTIN MACAULEY PUBLISHERS™
LONDON • CAMBRIDGE • NEW YORK • SHARJAH

Copyright © Innes Yates 2023

The right of Innes Yates to be identified as author of this work has been asserted by the author in accordance with sections 77 and 78 of the Copyright, Designs and Patents Act 1988.

All rights reserved. No part of this publication may be reproduced, stored in a retrieval system, or transmitted in any form or by any means, electronic, mechanical, photocopying, recording, or otherwise, without the prior permission of the publishers.

Any person who commits any unauthorised act in relation to this publication may be liable to criminal prosecution and civil claims for damages.

This is a work of fiction. Names, characters, businesses, places, events, locales and incidents are either the products of the author's imagination or used in a fictitious manner. Any resemblance to actual persons, living or dead, or actual events is purely coincidental.

A CIP catalogue record for this title is available from the British Library.

ISBN 9781035813797 (Paperback)
ISBN 9781035813803 (ePub e-book)

www.austinmacauley.com

First Published 2023
Austin Macauley Publishers Ltd®
1 Canada Square
Canary Wharf
London
E14 5AA

I would like to thank my wonderful family for their help with computer skills, typing manuscripts and proof reading as well as their continued support and encouragement.

# One

It was a hot, steamy day. In the field, two farm workers sat side by side on a stone wall, their bodies aching for a cool retreat. They were partly shaded by a small tree but there was really nowhere to find comfort in the intense heat. One man sank his white teeth into a piece of water melon. The juice ran down his chin, making its pathway between the lines of stubble, a day's growth, which crowned his weather beaten face. He wanted to rub it over his body, to drown in the cool but instead, he thirstily sucked from the pinky green mass while wiping drops of juice from his face with an earth-caked hand. The other man passed a bottle to him and he quenched his thirst while a fly scurried over his wrist then flew off. The afternoon stretched endlessly ahead.

The large limousine seemed to slither into the silent hamlet. The engine purred quietly while sunlight played games with the metallic surface, bringing it to life, first on the bonnet and then, as the car moved further over the dusty road, on the roof before gradually fading. Tyres caught the gravel, dried by the heat as it came to a halt outside the small hotel. Black looked at his watch. It was almost one o'clock. He had been driving for several hours. He stretched. His body was large, muscular and dark skinned like an apple which has ripened and dropped to the ground to be weathered. Beads of perspiration gathered on his forehead and his cotton shirt stuck to his skin, under his arms and across his chest. He felt uncomfortable and irritable as he opened the car door, the noise breaking in to the languid peace and vexing him more. Slamming the door behind him, he leaned through the open window and turned his head to the Blonde.

'Well, we're here, Baby. Better get the luggage out.'

He moved to the rear of the car.

She looked at him as though for the first time. Her eyes were blue and slightly sad, with a certain aura of hopelessness about them. She was a slight creature with an elfin face framed by almost white blonde hair which fell like silk to her shoulders. Her body was firm, ivory-coloured and her face was shielded against the sun by a large hat which protected her delicate skin from the heat. Quietly releasing the door, she allowed her foot to tentatively touch the surface of the gravel road, easing her body elegantly from the oven that was the car. The door clicked behind her as she faced the dilapidated hotel.

The front looked uninviting. It had once been painted white but the winter weather in these parts had blasted the brickwork to a crumbling mass and the summer suns had blistered the paintwork. Parts were flaking and decaying, revealing the bricks underneath. To her it looked as though no one had stayed here for many summers. Still she did not speak but made her way, slowly, nervously up the stone steps, wanting to turn back yet powerless to do so.

In a moment, Black was beside her, his strong arms round her waist, pulling her body insistently towards his. She could feel the warmth, feel the wetness of the sweat on his shirt and smell the muskiness of his body. She was gripped one moment with anticipation, the next with fear and guilt. His warm, sweet breath whispered quietly over her face, breathing life into her, firing her innermost self, giving birth to feelings which she knew were there but had lain dormant for so long. She responded, her body rising expectantly towards his as his mouth moved from the curve of her neck to the hollow of her ear, opening the door to her sensuality. His grip was hard, demanding as he buried his head amongst her hair. His lips, warm and moist, kissed her neck which was cool despite the heat all around them.

'Oh, Kitten,' he whispered in his soft American drawl, 'I've waited so long for this.'

Continuing to kiss her neck, moving round now to her cheek and brushing the hair back from her face, he turned the sculpted chin to where his lips met hers. His kiss was urgent, almost vicious, and she recoiled from the harshness of it for only a moment before submitting to the sea of euphoria in which she now swam. As much as she might have wanted to, it was now too late to turn back. The Blonde had crossed the threshold of her fantasies.

The room was cool. Black set down the luggage and surveyed the scene from the doorway. Behind him, the Blonde stood silent.

'Well, Honey, this is it! I think I'll have a quick shower to wake me after the long drive.'

And he turned from her to open his case. She looked at his broad back and a sense of pleasure ran through her. He was here with her at last. But as his suntanned arms delved into the expensive leather case, producing unfamiliar clothes, a feeling of strangeness and self-reproach overpowered her and stole her mood of contentment. Black found his washbag and disappeared into the adjoining bathroom.

The room seemed dominated by the large bed covered by a faded blue bedspread which clung loosely around its frame. She sat down and absent-mindedly smoothed the embossed surface of the cover with shiny pink nails. It felt rough under her hand and reminded her of the Jacquard loom designs she once made at Art College. Her studio had been taken on a special outing to a local factory with massive machines gurgling like monsters as they regurgitated metre after metre of patterned material from their mouths. She remembered the noise. Calamitous rhythmic clanking dominating the space. It was sore on the ears and the lecturer had to shout above it to be heard.

She thought about those days, her age of innocence when she had been catapulted from the security of home into an adult world. How naive she had been. How moral she had been, adept at positioning her arm just below her breast to ward off wandering hands. Then she thought about how stupid she had felt when her flatmates related their experiences and she couldn't join in. They had obviously welcomed the wandering hands and enjoyed their new found freedom. She remembered the teasing and yearned to know what they knew.

'You haven't done it, have you?'

'Still a virgin!'

'Not had any leg over!'

A redness crept over her cheeks as she remembered.

'We'll have to find her a guy!' they chorused and they did. He was tall and slim and blonde. Dan. He was twenty and in his second year of Medicine at the University. He was kind and shy, like her, and they bonded together in a ball of mutual solemnity. They read, they studied and they watched television while the others partied all night.

One weekend they found themselves alone in the flat, lying on her bed covered in the little bit of street lighting which filtered through the thin curtains. He held her close and they kissed. It was just a pressing of lips as he was as inexperienced as she was. But she saw her chance and encouraged him. Eventually she was lying in only her bra and pants and she touched his bare chest which was warm against hers. He was naked. She could feel his penis against her bare flesh. It was hard and smooth like a candle. They were two innocents fumbling in the darkness until he was inside her. When it was over, she did not feel as she had expected to feel. In fact, she just felt sore and disappointed. It had all been very robotic. Dan and she were not much more than friends. Their relationship was just a habit that was difficult to break. She longed for a time when she could feel real passion and even love.

An old bedside table filled the space to the window and a small lamp sat on top of this. She moved across the room and looked out over the field. Everything seemed silent. No sign of life anywhere in the yellow blue heaviness outside. Drawing the thin, cotton curtains, she lay down on the bed and sighed deeply. The wall paper was pale and old. A faint floral pattern surrounded her and she tried to imagine the fabric when it had been new. The faded, muted blues would have been vibrant then, giving a brightness to the room which it now lacked.

She closed her eyes for a moment and lazily arranged her legs into a sophisticated position on the bed, one stretched flat meeting the end of the bed, the other bent so that the calf of her leg hung loose and curved gracefully, sensually down to the elegant ankle. Quietly, she tossed the soft, leather sandals from her feet and they fell, discarded to the carpet below sending back a dull thud. The milk-white arms stretched above her head on the pillow and the blonde hair framed her face. She knew that she looked good and that was her intention.

Presently, Black emerged from the lighted bathroom. He was naked to the waist, a towel in one hand. A faint smell of aftershave wafted in front of him into the room. For an instant, he was dazzled while his eyes adjusted to the light. He blinked a few times, the long lashes gently touching his dried cheeks, and then he saw her. In the half light, she lay there, all inviting, like a goddess, one long line from head to toe of sculpted icing sugar, like the topping on a birthday cake his mother had made for him when he was a child. He smiled. At last she was here, alone with him, waiting for him but it was so hot. He dried his hands on the towel and buried his face in the thick material, momentarily taking his eyes from her.

Then he was beside her, his strong arms round her waist, the warmth of his body eating into her flesh. Light filtered through the chink in the curtains, casting shadows over their bodies as they lay entwined. The Blonde had often imagined this moment in the months which had passed but it had never seemed like this in her imagination. She had conjured up pictures of his lifestyle in America; of grand houses flanked by private swimming pools, of white-jacketed waiters serving chilled champagne carried on silver trays, their faces humourless, detached, as they performed their duties with professionalism. Black and the Blonde would laze beside the pool with a few carefully chosen people, some of whom would crave his friendship, and she would bask in his fame. Presently, as the sun dipped down behind the white marble walls of the villa, they would politely take their leave of the gathered entourage, climb the wide staircase to one of the many rooms where they would slither into a bed of the most expensive silk, the colour of her eyes, and make love until dawn. The dream had not become reality.

She lay in his arms like a puppet, her body loose and light. A river of excitement flowed through her. At last she could feel his naked body next to hers. She held her breath. Urgently, he manipulated her beneath him and moving between her thighs, she felt the pulsating, warmth of him inside her. Tentatively at first them positively, demanding. He seemed to be squeezing the breath from her body but she did not want it to stop. This was passion. This was what she had craved all these years and the dreams fled from her head, no longer of any importance as she submitted to the reality, their shadows eventually undulating rhythmically to a halt.

'Gee, Honey, you're gorgeous,' he sighed, pressing her body in a final thrust of emotion. He kissed her warm cheeks and swept back the hair now clinging moistly round her face. The Blonde felt light headed as he lay inside her, his emotions spent. They felt good having tasted the realisation of their hopes over the past few months.

In the distant field, two farm workers were stripped to the waist, their golden bodies glistening amongst the fresh, yellow corn. Sweat ran in rivulets down the curve of their backs and shimmered in the strong sun as they lifted bales of hay and stacked them in the open field. The sun was all powerful, the heat unbearable but they laboured on. Every other creature in the area had sought the shade. There was no other activity around except the farmer on his tractor further afield, the engine's drone adding a low, menacing murmur to the scene.

She woke quietly, her eyes blinking against the blades of bright light cutting across her pillow. He lay next to her and, as she turned to find him, realised through her sleepiness that he was already awake and looking at her. He smiled slowly, a knowing smile revealing strong, white teeth and a firm mouth. Drawing her finger over his lips, she kissed them. They lay in silence for some time, just enjoying their new found intimacy, sometimes smiling, kissing and caressing.

Later, she prepared herself for the day. She creamed her pale cheeks and brushed her thick hair, feeling its heaviness between her fingers. Remorse suddenly engulfed her as she caught sight of her near naked body, framed in a long mirror in unfamiliar surroundings. She looked at a face still young, still beautiful which had attracted many men but few of whom had managed to crack her icy exterior to sample the favours of her warm being. She thought briefly about her husband but the weight of her deception was too much so she quickly dismissed his image from her mind. Once she had loved him but that had been a long time ago. Now their relationship had turned sour and, for her, there was nothing left to salvage. She could no longer maintain the pretence. Soon. It would have to be soon.

They strolled in the early morning sunshine, arms around each other. The dewy flagstones printed their footsteps as they walked into the silence and reached their car. Large tinted sunglasses hid part of her face, the china-glazed features small and elfin under the obtrusive frames. Black held open a door for her then they screeched off, scattering the early birds from their roadside perches while the tractor lay dormant at the edge of the field. Black put a strong hand on top of hers and smiled. The day lay ahead of them like an unopened book.

They walked along the edge of the yellow field, down to the lake where they swam, laughed and teased each other. He was strong, coaxing and dominant and she enjoyed the domination. She was coy at times, reticent, appealing and remorseful. It was all a game but it mattered for that moment in time and she suddenly realised why he had brought her here, to the broken-down hotel. Here was absolute peace, absolute release, absolute anonymity, where they could learn about each other.

The sun was rising high in the sky now, sending down searing tails of yellow heat as they lay beside the lake, lazing in the warmth. The fields stretched for miles around them and they appeared as two dots by the waterside to a plane which flew overhead.

He held her now, kissing the shoulder heated by the sun and sculpted by her mother's body. She wriggled beneath him encouragingly and his lips found hers warm and tempting. His hand slowly found her bikini top and released it from her body. For a moment she felt vulnerable, naked, but the sun heated her and inhibitions were overtaken by feelings of expectancy.

They kissed, slowly at first, then more urgently. His hand caressed her thigh and now she felt is fingers slip the bottom of her bikini lower, revealing everything. When he touched her she felt electrified. She did not care where they were, all sense of time and presence being lost. She was ready, eager to taste him again and she felt the same pleasure as yesterday as he slid inside her, penetrating her innermost depths. This time there were no feelings of guilt. It was all so easy now and together they moved in rhythm.

Distant gun shots could be heard. Beside them, a bird flew low over the lake, noisily flapping its wings, beating into the warm air. Crack…crack…crack…as his wing tips skimmed the water's surface in his bid for freedom. Black and the Blonde did not notice the bird's escape.

The weekend was over too soon but the Blonde had savoured every moment in the knowledge that these illicit interludes might not last. She supposed she was in love. In fact she had difficulty analysing what love meant but she imagined that it was a state of mind which endured all ills and she was unsure if she had ever been in that situation.

At the moment, her life was exciting, the ever increasing pulse of discovery beating in their every gesture, an added zing to her life which helped to block out the daily tedium. Already a fresh, peachy flush had sneaked into her cheeks and a new vibrancy coloured her blue eyes. Her walk incorporated a new confidence which she had never felt within the confines of her marriage.

They left the countryside behind. Sun reflected in their eyes, yellow fields flashed by, trees lush with greenery swayed at their passing as the engine droned along the lanes. Black skilfully manipulated the car round corners and over crossings. Soon the scene changed as they entered the edge of London.

Grey buildings with dark windows lined the road, factories, shops all closed on this sultry Sunday, their occupants engaged in different pastimes, relaxing their work-worn bodies before the rigours of the coming week.

The traffic was heavy, the junctions dappled with cars of every colour bearing families returning from weekend visits. Pairs of youths hung their sunburnt arms from car windows as they admired legs on the sidewalk and wanted to be admired in return, their thumping music acting as a beacon. Elderly couples taking a drive in the countryside were returning and the Blonde supposed there would be people like themselves who had snatched a few hours together before returning to their monotonous lives.

She felt empty now. Soon they would say goodbye and she was dreading that moment. She hoped that he would want to see her again but the waiting, the living from day to day in between, would be unbearable. If only she could have him now for an extended period of time, she could extinguish the fire within her and return to some state of normality.

Black drew the car to a halt outside the Tube Station and, turning to her, put his arm round her shoulder.

'Thank you for a wonderful weekend, Kitten!' He kissed her cheek and looked at her in silence then said dismissively, 'I'll ring you.'

The door clicked closed behind her and he drew away from the pavement, not looking back at the slim figure outlined against the landscape of people. She watched his silhouette dim against the glare of the windscreen as he disappeared into the rush of traffic. She felt dismissed and deflated. Was it possible she had imagined that Black felt the same as she did? Their parting had been unemotional but what did she expect? Perhaps he was afraid that he might be recognised and needed a quick getaway. Thoughts spun through her mind. He would ring but when? The waiting would be painful. Then she remembered that she was married and had obligations whereas he had none. He was free to do as he wanted. She had no claim on him.

It seemed as though the weekend had never happened, surrounded as she was by disinterested crowds pushing to get tickets, running to catch trains and eager to return home. The Blonde was not eager to get home but she slowly resigned herself to the fact that this was the reality and it had to be lived. She was going home a different woman to the one who had left there two days before. Thinking about Black gave her a feeling of warmth and hope but she would have to be careful to suppress this in case Philip suspected.

Her key turned silently in the lock and opened the door of their house. She set her case on the tiled floor and quietly surveyed the paintings which lined the wall on either side of the large hallway. They seemed somehow unfamiliar to her, jaded and worn, their colours lacking lustre as though they were born from another life. An antique table stood sentinel at the foot of the wide stairway where a grandfather clock ticked quietly, eating into the silence and mingling in time with the trembling of her body. It struck her how strange all these objects were, as though she were viewing them for the first time.

The television mumbled incoherently from the first room to the left of the hallway. He would be there watching it, an atmosphere of gloom surrounding him. For months they had hardly spoken. The Blonde could not establish exactly what had gone wrong or when but eventually they had escalated into a relationship in which they chose to live together in disharmony. It was a bitter liaison at times and at others, almost affable but to her, always unacceptable.

For a moment, he did not look at her when she entered the room. The Blonde's insides turned over afraid that somehow her guilt had changed her physically and he would recognise it.

'How is your sister?' he asked, a stony expression on his face. She froze and then remembered. Turning away and removing her jacket, she sat on the sofa, legs crossed elegantly and lit a cigarette. She did not look in his direction.

'She's much better. Sitting up in bed now. The doctor said she should be able to get up in a day or two.'

She surveyed his face looking for a trace of disbelief but it was so expressionless that it was difficult to know if he believed her or not. The silence was heavy, broken only by the background noise of the television. She wondered if he would ask any more questions about Leonie but he stared ahead, his dishevelled hair not brushed, the odd streak of grey catching the light. She thought how boring he looked in his conventional trousers which hung loose over his lean frame. His face was gaunt, the cheeks hollow and the eyes blue and lifeless.

She tried to remember what had first attracted her to Philip and was transported to that night they first met. Leonie and her husband, Jeff, had invited her to dinner. Leonie had said, with an impish look, that they had someone they would like her to meet. The rendezvous was the Grosvenor Hotel and the four sat in luxurious surroundings, eating, drinking and laughing. She found him attractive, humorous and talkative and by the end of the evening the Blonde and Philip had discovered an affinity—art. It drew them together. It was comforting like lying in a warm bath.

His lifestyle and artistic nature had suited hers. He was a designer of some talent based in Central London. He knew everyone. He had seemed so busy, so full of vitality then. He knew everyone and seemed to go everywhere. Each day had been different, filled with surprises, new people, and social events. Their life had been one huge round of activity, but then things had changed when they married. The Blonde thought they would continue as before but more and more he refused invitations and became a semi-recluse, wishing only the quiet life and hoping for children to complete that life. She felt imprisoned and he became her gaoler.

She carried her small suitcase to the bedroom. The room felt icy and a shiver ran through her body as she removed her outer garments. She did not hear his footsteps which were muffled by the thick pile carpet. He stood behind her, hands in pockets.

'I'm glad you're back,' he said quietly, trying to smile. She didn't respond. Suddenly, sickeningly, his arms enclosed her body from behind. They were cold and his actions sent a more powerful tremor through her.

'Are you cold?' he asked as his lips brushed her neck and his hands rose higher, encasing her breasts. She could tell he wanted her but did not answer. Revulsion and hatred rose inside her yet guilt at what she had done. Perhaps she owed him something so she resigned herself to what was about to happen.

He tried to be charming, loveable, to win her back as though everything between them was wonderful. He needed her desperately. It had been so long. As he moved sporadically on top of her she tried to remember him as he had been when they first met but her fingernails dug into his smooth flesh, nearly drawing blood. Soon it was over and he lay on top of her, satiated. She wondered how she could submit to this, allow it to happen so soon after leaving Black. He rolled over on the bed, exhausted, and soon she could hear the rhythmic breathing of sleep.

She tip-toed to the door carefully turning the brass handle. The door creaked on its hinges and she stood motionless for a second, holding her breath, convinced the noise would waken him but he slept soundly.

Making her way down the long, turning staircase, she quietly opened a door leading to the back of the house. This was his study. Here he spent most of his time. It was his domain and she felt like a trespasser as she made her way to the chair behind his tidy desk. She took her mobile from her dressing gown pocket and, fingers trembling, pressed the number. It rang once, then again. She waited, shaking from the cold atmosphere, her breathing eating into the silence.

'Hello,' a voice answered.

'Leonie,' she whispered, 'It's me.'

'Can you speak up? I can hardly hear you!' Her sister shouted from the other end. Glancing over her shoulder at the door, the Blonde cleared her throat as silently as she could and repeated, 'It's me, Leonie. I've got to see you! Can I come tomorrow on the first train?'

'Oh, I can hear you now. Of course you can! Why the hell are you whispering? Is everything alright?'

'I can't talk now. I'll see you tomorrow.' She quickly ended the call.

# Two

Leonie lived by the sea now and the journey by train seemed interminable. It rained after the steamy weekend and water run in rivulets down the windows, slashing them into sections, cutting pictures of the ever-changing landscape into jigsaw pieces. Thunder rolled overhead and it was still hot and humid.

The Blonde stepped from the taxi which had taken her from the station. Above, lightening flashed in ever increasing intensity as her umbrella shielded her from the deluge which splashed over the sides and tumbled down her legs, running in between her toes, exposed through the bars of her sandals. She ran up the path of the rambling house, stumbling here and there on the cobbles while over hanging roses, drooping from the cloudburst, soaked her skirt and threw spray into her face. She fumbled for the boor bell, dropping her bag on the stone step. Almost immediately the door opened, throwing out an aroma of freshly made coffee.

'My God, you're soaked!' Leonie said as the Blonde stood bedraggled, dripping onto the parquet flooring, pools of water forming round her feet. 'Run upstairs and change out of those wet clothes,' her sister ordered. 'You certainly chose the wrong day to visit! I'll get you a pair of my jeans to wear…and put that umbrella in the bath!'

She dried her hair, and slid into the well-worn jeans Leonie had found for her then made her way downstairs.

'What a day' she sighed as she dropped heavily into one of the kitchen chairs. It was a large space—two rooms knocked into one with a low beamed ceiling. French windows stood open in the far wall, leading onto a large, paved patio beyond which grew gigantic Mountain Ash which surrounded the house. In the distance, a child's swing and paddling pool lay deserted. Rain spattered the surface of the pool where dead flies floated, moved continually by the force of the downpour. Summer was being transformed.

Leonie fussed around her sister, pouring fresh coffee into china mugs while the rain lashed ferociously against the windows, interspersed with flashes of lightning. She finally sat down and for the first time, the Blonde noticed her sister had been crying.

'Are you alright?' she asked, stretching her hand over to Leonie's. She looked tired, the fine features older now and her hair drawn back from her forehead accentuating her empty stare. Leonie was silent for a moment and sat looking at her hands. Her fingers played with the spoon in the sugar bowl, endlessly turning over the brown granules, making ridges with the edge then smoothing them over again.

'No! I'm not alright!' she said slowly, 'I don't know if I ever will be again! Jeff's left me!' She looked incredulously at her sister, hysteria slowly mounting inside her.

'Left you? Oh, Leonie! I'm so sorry…' The Blonde was silenced.

'He's staying up at the cottage in Norfolk to sort himself out,' Leonie muttered, her voice thin and helpless. 'I thought once it had finished he would forget her and we could be a family again, just like we used to be…but it hasn't worked out like that. I suppose I was hoping for too much!' and she snatched her hand from the Blonde's and wiped back tears. The Blonde ran to her sister and held her.

'Oh, Leonie! I thought things between you were good. I'd no idea…'

'Good!' Leonie laughed hysterically, pushing her away, 'My God, what do you know! It's been absolute hell since that bitch got her claws into him. I could kill her! She's ruined all we ever worked for and now he's left me, the kids, everything because of her, the bloody cow!' She started weeping again but more violently, her hands covering her face, her back heaving as she gave way to her frustrated anger.

'I can't believe it! How did it happen?'

'How does it always happen? I didn't go to one of the studio functions and she had free range. Seemingly, she pursued him for weeks, determined to get him into bed and she finally managed it. She's one of those women who want something she doesn't have but in the end, when she gets it, throws it away like an old toy she's grown tired of.' She paused. 'He can't forget her, you know. As soon as he told her he was leaving me, she buggered off to pastures new, couldn't face the thought of being tied down. God, he's such a bloody fool, nearly old enough to be her father and couldn't see that she was just a flighty piece, not worth sacrificing everything for.'

She wiped her face with a crumpled tissue and stood up from the table. She began preparing lunch. The salad was washed. She poured oil and vinegar into a bowl, hardly aware of what she was doing. Then she fumbled with the top of the mustard container and sprinkled some into the mixture.

'Let me help you,' the Blonde said, attempting to grip the bowl but Leonie pushed her away.

'No! I can do it myself!' and she started to whipt the mixture viciously.

Leonie laid the salad in a daisy patterned dish and lovingly ran her finger along the edge of it, remembering.

'Ironic! This dish was a wedding present all those years ago and now it's survived longer than us!' She paused, remembering. 'It wouldn't be so bad but he doesn't want me any longer. I'm just a reject, been discarded, and don't merit a look in compared to this hot bit of stuff he's had! It really hurts. Please God I never meet her face to face!' And she released her venom, beating the salad dressing, tears mingling with the oil in the bowl. The Blonde was shocked. She felt powerless. She thought about Jeff and never imagined that he could ever leave Leonie. Jeff the father. Jeff the conventional man.

The sun now shone outside with great ferocity, the storm having passed. Leonie flung open the French windows further and breathed in the fresh air. In the distance, the sea moved rapidly, angry waves throwing white foam onto the beach. Seagulls swarmed noisily, disturbing the surrounding stillness. Leonie watched them in silence. It gave her a chance to compose herself before turning to her younger sister.

'Anyway, enough about me,' she tried a reluctant smile, 'Why all the mystery on the 'phone last night?' She scrutinised her sister's face while the Blonde thought that it was an inappropriate time to tell her about Black but it burned inside her. It had to come out. She had to tell someone.

'I've met this man,' she said simply, her voice hardly audible.

'Met a man? What man?' Leonie asked incredulously.

'It doesn't matter who he is. All that matters is that I've met him. I told Philip that I was staying with you last weekend but in actual fact...' She hesitated, reluctant to continue with her admission, 'I spent the weekend with him.'

There was a black silence then a whispered, 'My God!' from Leonie. She stopped what she was doing, laid the salad aside and stared at the Blonde. 'I hope you know what you're doing! What about Phillip? Who is he? Do you love him?'

There were too many questions. The Blonde shrugged. She rose from the table and moved across to lean against the frame of the French windows, her hands sunk deeply into the pockets of Leonie's old jeans. The sun was hot now and steam rose from the concrete paving stones as the heat dried the remains of the rain. She could see the sea in the distance, feel the salt on her lips and watch the waves trying to cling to the shore before being buffeted back to try again.

'Does it really matter if I love him?' she asked tentatively, looking far beyond the skyline, 'I love being with him. He wants me and I want him and I love him wanting me!' She turned to look at her sister. 'I can't go on living with Philip without some release.'

Leonie did not look up.

'Release? Is that what they call it now?'

Her face showed no emotion. Suddenly, a horrendous shattering noise exploded as Leonie hurled the daisy dish against the wall. Salad leaves sat in suspended animation before floating quietly to the floor. Nothing moved except Leonie's lips which spat out 'Bastards!'

The Blonde knelt down and started to pick up the cracked pieces. She had never seen her elder sister like this. Only three years separated them but she had always looked up to her as Leonie had always been calm and in control.

'Leave it!' Leonie screamed. 'Just leave it!'

'But...'

'You're a bloody fool, you know! You never did know what you felt. What if Philip finds out? Have you thought about that or don't you care? Don't' you care about your lifestyle... your home? You're putting all that in jeopardy. Thank God you don't have children. At least that's one thing to be thankful for.' She hesitated. 'Do you realise you are as bad as Jeff?' Her voice was firm and even now. 'You've both been unfaithful! Philip and I don't deserve it! We're innocent victims! What if he finds out and leaves you?'

The Blonde listened and then grew angry. She did not accept that Philip was an innocent victim.

'I don't think Philip would leave me even if he did find out!' Her voice was raised. 'He loves me and wants me to love him but at the moment, I can't!'

'What do you mean, 'at the moment'? It's not something you can turn on and off!' she snarled, 'It's got to be worked at, to be nurtured! It's got to grow in strength!' She ran her fingers through her hair in exasperation.

'Look, Leonie,' the blonde cried, 'I can't live with Philip unless he meets me half way. God knows I've tried. One moment he's up and the next he's down. I never know which mood I'm going to find him in and I can't stand these continual changes. Do you hear me, I can't stand them!' She banged the table with her hand. 'The more I've tried to love him, the more difficult it's become. He sets obstacles in my path all the way. He emotionally blackmails me into bed, otherwise he won't speak to me, just closes me out. You've no idea what a hell it is living with him.'

She sat down at the table opposite her sister. They sat in silence. Too much had been said. Eventually, Leonie asked, 'When did this start?'

The Blonde sighed, reluctant to continue the conversation.

'About a year ago when I told him I didn't want to have children. You know how much he wants a family. I just don't want to be bull-dozed into it. I'm the one who is going to be carrying a baby for nine months, give birth to it and will virtually be its slave until God knows when yet his life would hardly be touched…hardly changed at all. I'm not ready for that type of responsibility and I don't know if I ever will be.'

'Perhaps it's just that you don't love Philip enough,' said Leonie.

'Perhaps,' said the Blonde, 'Perhaps it's as easy to fall out of love as it is to fall in love.'

'In lust, you mean!' said Leonie bitterly.

Neither of them felt like eating. The chicken had survived and lay untouched beside their empty plates. The sun squeezed through the French windows, lighting up part of the kitchen and a heaviness fell on the two women as afternoon slipped into evening.

'Why don't you let Philip go?' Leonie asked, her voice somehow detached, flat, a thin echo. The Blonde thought for a moment.

'It's not as simple as that. He doesn't want to go.'

'Well, you'll just have to live with it!' shouted Leonie, her own bitterness surfacing once more.

'It's not enough!' The Blonde stood up from the table and collected her handbag. 'That's why there IS another man. Look, I'd better go…I'm sorry about things between you and Jeff. If only there was something I could do…'

'There's nothing anyone can do! I'll just have to wait… see if time changes things. Philip won't see him around the studios for a while. Perhaps you would tell him why.'

She looked at Leonie, sitting all alone and wanted to hug her, to put her arms round her neck like they used to do when they were children but there was now a deep rift between them. Instead, she kissed her briefly on the cheek. There was no response so she turned to leave and said, 'I'll tell him.'

She stepped into the taxi. Her clothes were dry again. Leonie stood framed in the door, thin and sad. She suffocated tears which wanted to surface as the taxi roared over the cobbled road, throwing her against the window and ricocheting her back to the depths of the seat. Soon she was on the train and realised that the whole effect of the day's visit to her sister had totally drained her. She resolved to think about nothing except Black so that she could soothingly bathe in memories of the weekend. She thought back to the first time they met. It had started innocently enough. Phillip had decided to attend one of the studio functions, not because he wanted to socialise particularly, but because he hoped to design the sets for a new television show later in the year and the actor involved would be attending.

The party was being held to celebrate the opening of the film, 'The Wasp' starring Eduardo Costello, a well-known box-office success. The room was crowded with directors, producers, actors and hangers-on.

The Blonde felt the excitement steal into her bones, a feeling which these occasions always invoked in her. She became alive again. It had been so long since she and Philip had attended one of these social gatherings and she never tired of studying the people and listening to snippets of conversations, some of which were pure platitudes. She smiled inwardly. Eduardo Costello stood taller than most in the room, enjoying the limelight in the centre of a group of people who all wished to please him. They struggled to gain his attention even for a fleeting moment, merely to taste his fame.

His hair was blonde, streaked with grey, his skin deeply tanned and his eyes, piercing blue. But it was not Eduardo who attracted her attention. At the other side of the crowded studio, she saw a man as tall as Eduardo Costello, also surrounded by an adoring crowd. His eyes met hers and both of them stood motionless, staring at each other until someone at his side repeated his question of a moment before and he turned, apologising but in a moment his gaze again strayed in her direction. It was as though they recognised each other but she had never seen him before. Her stomach flipped over. No man had ever had this effect on her. It was as if an invisible magnet drew them together.

'Yes! There he is!' cried Phillip excitedly. 'Black Lomax. He's the guy I told you about. I want to work on the sets for his television show.'

'Who is he?' whispered the Blonde, as much to herself as Phillip. Her excitement gnawed at her insides until she could hardly contain it.

'He's Eduardo Costello's co-star in 'The Wasp'. Seemingly, he's going to be big.'

Pushing his way through the crowd, Phillip reached Black Lomax. For a moment, his gaze was lost to her. Heads and shoulders moved between them in a continuous over-lapping movement obscuring her view. Eventually, she could see Phillip talking to Black and then they made their way towards her, weaving together through clumps of noisy, laughing people, some sipping drinks while others blew thin threads of smoke from cigarettes into the already thick air. Sometimes the crowd moved apart to let a waiter pass and she caught a glimpse of his young, handsome face. Then he was standing in front of her, his firm mouth set in a smile. They shook hands and a warmth ran through her. She held his firm shake for just a moment too long. She was speechless, naked before him and she could tell that he sensed this. She felt that he could read her thoughts. They were both aware of the intense attraction between them and the Blonde thought that she had never seen such a beautiful man. Something inside her knew that she would not rest until she had satisfied her curiosity.

Someone called to Phillip from the other side of the room. He excused himself saying that he needed to talk to them urgently. Black Lomax turned to the Blonde. At last he could look at her undisturbed and he allowed himself the pleasure of testing his own attractiveness. But something about her disturbed him and Black could not understand why his usual feeling of confidence, when faced with a new conquest, had left him.

'I'm told your husband's quite some guy where sets are concerned.'

He looked at her questioningly. His American accent was both rich and captivating. Both knew that Phillip was not really what they wanted to talk about. The game had begun.

'Yes,' she muttered almost incoherently, afraid of the sound of her own voice, 'He's had quite a bit of experience.'

'How…?'

They both began talking at the same time to break the silence which followed the last answer and they laughed.

'After you!' he joked, throwing back a thick head of curly, black hair.

'I was just going to ask you a rather mundane question such as, 'how long are you intending to stay over here?' and she laughed with him.

'Well, let's say that rather depends. It depends on a lot of things,' he replied, becoming rather serious, his eyes fixing hers as he pointedly repeated the last few words, '…on a lot of things.'

For the remainder of the evening, he never left her side, making it very clear to those who were eager to talk, that he was already engaged in conversation and did not welcome an intrusion. And so it began.

When Phillip returned, Black told him that they would have to meet up soon to discuss business. This way, she knew she would see him again. Neither of them, lost in their growing togetherness, saw the redhead, her hair a long, shimmering mass of auburn lights, her penetrating green eyes, as keen as a cat's, scrutinising their every move. She lurked in the background, in the dark shadows, watching, waiting, like a tigress cunningly stalking her prey.

# Three

July died quietly. The sun lingered supreme throughout that month and still burned strongly into August. The Blonde wandered around the large house, her movements disturbing the emptiness as the sun slipped through the open windows, warming the polished surfaces. In the distance, the slow, pulsating noise of traffic could be heard on the busy street. The occasional car horn sounded, breaking the over powering monotony. A wasp lazily flew through the open window adding a new noise to the scene. It buzzed back and forth trying to find an escape from its self-inflicted imprisonment. Her mobile rang crushing the tranquillity.

'Phillip here.' The voice was distant, abrupt. She could picture him in his office, shirt sleeves rolled against the heat, his face set firmly, 'I've invited Black Lomax back for a drink tonight. You remember him, don't you?' and, without waiting for an answer, 'We want to discuss some details for the sets on his programme. See you later.'

Her hand shook as she put down her mobile. She felt chilled. Black coming here...this evening? Images passed through her head. She had waited for his call but it never came so she had dismissed their night together as a one-off, nothing more on his part. She sat down, dazed. How could she face him in her home environment with Phillip there? She hadn't yet come to terms with the situation. She needed time to think, consider, and maybe decide.

Water rushed out of the taps, sending spirals of steam hurtling upwards, entangling each other in a ghostly dance until they reached the ceiling and died. Bubbles of green foam, pine scented, lived for a moment on the water's surface before bursting and making way for others, some smaller, in their thousands like pin heads and some the size of eggs. She watched them float to the surface reflecting the images around her, distorting their shapes and colours, mirroring her face for a second before exploding.

Dropping her towel to the ground, she stepped into the bath, slipping her toes und0er the blanket of bubbles, feeling the coolness of the enamel against her body and the warmth of the water above. It smelt nice. A perfumed smoothness enveloped her, soaking into every pore, relaxing her tense muscles.

She could think clearly now. Nearly a month had passed since she had last seen him. Trying to picture his face in her mind was difficult. She could only recall parts. It was like a jigsaw puzzle. First the eyes, then she tried to imagine his nose and mouth and when they were almost within her grasp, they would fade, evading her. She lay this way for some time, soaking in the memories of their last weekend and enjoying the exciting, expectant feeling which it gave her. Over the last few weeks, she had longed for him to ring but he never did. It had been agony for her and she began to doubt herself. Was she his latest conquest, tasted then forgotten? Had she imagined that they shared more than that?

Later she dressed. Nothing outrageous, just a simple cream shift which clung to her outline. She felt confident in the dress, knowing that she looked good. Her hair shone like a halo round her faintly flushed face. It was tied back exposing her faultless features, the lips pink and moist as though the last strokes of an artist's brush had left them moments before. Smoothing her hand over the ivory cheeks, she surveyed her image. Her bare legs were long and slim and bronzed from the sun. Yes, this was the best she could do and she was pleased with the overall effect.

She had difficulty relating to the thoughts which sped through her mind. These thoughts were abruptly brought to an end. She could hear a key turning in the lock of the large oak door and then voices in the hallway. She stopped breathing and listened. Very faintly she could hear the soft, familiar drawl of Black's voice interspersed with Phillip's clipped business-like conversation. She moved slowly and waited for a moment before making her way downstairs.

'You remember Black?'

He stood in front of her, smiling, taller than Phillip, his blue eyes penetrating her soul. He seemed to dominate the space and a feeling which started in her stomach rose to her throat overwhelming her.

'Yes,' she said softly, her cheeks touched with pink. She moved towards him and clasped his outstretched hand. She remembered his touch and trembled inside in case Phillip noticed the unmistakeable look of intimacy which had passed between them.

'Nice to meet you again,' he smiled. He said it with ease as though he were playing a part. It was all too easy for him.

'Well, sit down Black. It's great to see you again. What would you like to drink?'

'Gee, that would be very nice. I'll have Scotch on the Rocks, please.'

Philip turned to the Blonde. She searched his face looking for a sign that he was suspicious but, as ever, he remained impassive and cold like the marble of some inanimate building built centuries before. He looked towards her.

'Drink?' he gestured with the glass which was in his hand.

'Whisky and ginger, please.' She replied hurriedly. She needed a drink, something strong. Anything would do. He looked at her disapprovingly and moved towards the drinks cabinet, busying himself putting ice and drinks in glasses. He was impatient, eager to continue his meeting.

Black sat opposite her and stared, devouring every part of her with his rich, blue eyes. She knew what he was doing and deliberately averted her gaze as she thought he was playing a dangerous game. Her impulse was to rush over and hold him but she knew it had to be curbed.

'Well, Black,' Philip handed round the drinks while continuing a conversation which was obviously started earlier, 'I think if we concentrate on the Spy Theme which, let's face it, is your trademark at the moment, we could produce something really dramatic.'

Black nodded disinterestedly and sipped from his glass. He hardly averted his eyes from the Blonde and it was making her uncomfortable. She gulped the amber liquid from her glass, then had another, forcing it across her throat. It slipped down easily now, warming her whole body.

As she had dreaded, Philip left them alone for a moment while he went to his study to search for photographs of sets which Black could browse through. As the door closed behind him, Black was beside her on the sofa.

'Why did you come here?' she asked, almost desperately, 'Phillip will realise!'

'I had to come! It seemed so long...' He stopped in mid-sentence, pulled her towards him and kissed her, pressing his body against hers, arousing feelings in the Blonde which she had been trying to suppress. She responded at first then remembered Phillip and pushed him away reluctantly, fear in her heart.

'For Christ sake,' she hissed, 'Do you know what you're doing?'

'I don't care,' he replied, 'I've gotta see you soon!'

They could hear Phillip's approaching footsteps in the hall and Black sprang back to his original seat.

She crossed quickly to the drinks cabinet then refilled Black's glass before pouring herself another and drinking it in one. The whole evening began to seem like a nightmare. She had never imagined Black in her familiar surroundings, sitting in the richly furnished lounge, with Persian carpets which she had chosen. It seemed sacrilege somehow. Her dream had become cruel reality. She looked at the antique chairs with their sumptuous satin cushions next to the huge ornate marble fireplace which housed an enormous fire in winter. She could imagine the flames dancing and mocking her. These were her possessions. This was her domain. This was her guilt. She felt light headed and dizzy, the whisky having taken effect.

'Mind if I use the John?' Black stood up and looked questioningly at Phillip.

'Of course. It's upstairs,' he replied. At that moment, the doorbell rang. 'Please excuse me. I'll answer that and Rachael will show you where it is.'

She climbed the stairs with Black close behind. They could hear Phillip open the front door.

'I'm sorry to bother0 you, Phillip, but I've got a flat tyre and have a shift at the hospital in half an hour. Do you have a Jack I could use?'

It was David, the doctor who lived next door. As they rounded the top of the stairs, they could hear Phillip saying he would get one from his garage. Barely out of sight, Black manipulated her gently against the wall and kissed her passionately.

'I want you now!' he whispered. Her stomach turned over like a waterwheel. She could hardly breathe in case Phillip heard. Black's strong hands moved up under her cream shift and encased her naked buttocks. She trembled with anticipation. He pulled her towards him and she could feel his fingers exploring, higher and higher, the inside of her thigh. He was teasing her and the more he teased, the hotter she became for him. Her excitement mounted, her breathing, rapid. Phillip shouted up the stairs.

'I'm going to help David. It's an emergency. So sorry. Be back as soon as possible.'

She could only manage a strangled acknowledgement as the front door closed behind him. A moment later, she felt the pulsating warmth of Black inside her. They moved quietly in unison at first then more urgently as they realised the house was theirs and they wouldn't be disturbed. Their movements increased in impetus until both settled back against the wall in a final burst of lust. She laughed nervously.

'Did that really just happen?'

Black said nothing. He smiled, kissed her cheek briefly then walked towards the bathroom. The Blonde rushed to her bedroom to check that her dress, hair and make-up were looking normal. Her face was slightly flushed but apart from that, Phillip would never suspect what had just happened in his house.

When she arrived downstairs, Black was already sitting on a sofa talking to Phillip who was apologising for the interruption. Neither of them looked up when she entered but continued discussing their business. She sat down on a chair and studied Black wondering how he could have instigated what happened. *'I want you now!'* His words kept slithering into her brain. It had been exciting at the time. No one had ever said that to her before and she was not sure if she liked it. Was she merely a nice distraction and was he pissing on Phillip's territory like an alley cat? The whole episode seemed disconnected from what she imagined they had shared before. She wondered how much she actually knew him.

Philip closed the door behind Black and she went to bed. She could hear him downstairs clearing glasses and closing windows. She wished she was asleep but sleep evaded her. Tossing the duvet aside, she rolled over on the starched pillow, a drum beating in her head, pounding out a message which she tried in vain to translate. Suddenly the room became awash with light as she heard him switch on the bedside light. She tried to open her eyes against it.

'What the hell…?' She muttered.

He sat up in bed and looked down at her. His higher position seemed to give him authority in her stupefied mind.

'What's it all about?' he asked coldly, confronting her when he could clearly see that she had a hangover. She did not want to speak, to discuss, only to sleep and forget, hoping that somehow the whole episode would disappear from her life and she could continue as before. But could she? Would sleep erase everything and could she start again? She doubted it and so she asked, 'What's what all about?'

'Us?' he answered sharply.

'Oh, God!' she groaned, 'Do we have to discuss this now, at this hour?' and tried to turn away, screwing up her eyes against the light which seemed more powerful than usual.

'Well, shit, we've got to discuss it sometime! We never have sex anymore!' She winced at the word. 'You never communicate with me. Don't you feel anything for me now?'

The beating in her head continued, adopting a tempo increasingly faster. In the silence which followed she was only aware of a question which had to be answered.

'Of course I care for you,' she grunted dismissively.

'But do you love me?' he insisted.

In the silence that followed, she could sense his rejection. He turned away and she could feel his devastation. They lay in quietness for a while then Phillip started to interrogate her again.

'And why all the drink? Don't you like Black Lomax or something…or are you so much in awe of him, he makes you nervous?'

She was fearful and pretended to be asleep. She could not ignore the feeling of panic which had engulfed her body. Never before had she managed to say it and now it was out. She could not live a lie yet she did not want him to leave her, not yet. Was she capable of living without him? It was a big step to take. Leonie's words hit back at her. 'What about your lifestyle? All that you've built up? Your home?' Six years was a long time. She knew his strengths and weaknesses and wore them like a comfortable coat. No fear of the unknown. No risk.

Yet Phillip seemed to be pushing her towards the precipice with constant questioning, forcing her to say things she did not mean to say. Or was it just that she had drunk too much and the alcohol had dulled her brain. She was sure that must be the reason. Sleep and in the morning it would be the same as usual. He would never leave her. It was understood between them. They were meant to stay together. Presently, she drifted off, her body comfortably next to his.

# Four

Philip stood hunched over his desk, hands in pockets. He could not concentrate on anything. He hadn't slept well last night. Running his fingers through his already dishevelled hair, he sighed deeply and sat down heavily on the chair at his desk.

'Damn her!' he uttered aloud, recalling the object of his mental and physical frustration. But deep down inside, he did not really mean it. It was impossible to continue the way they had been, he could see that, but still he saw her face before him and wondered how he would ever be able to remove her from his life. Somehow it would never be the same without her. Perhaps he was growing old, he thought, yet forty was supposed to be a beginning. If he gave her a bit more time to catch up with him, then it might work but he really did not believe that himself. He loved the Blonde but he knew that was not enough for her.

The redhead swaggered along the corridor, leisurely reading the names on each door. Inwardly, she thanked her father for finding her this job. For once, Daddy had been of some use. It was perfect timing and much more interesting than sunning herself on a beach in the south of France. That became boring after a while.

Philip looked up, startled. He wasn't expecting anyone. His thoughts had been disturbed and he was torn back to reality. Silently she came towards him, her body seeming to slither across the floor, one complete undulation of womanhood, perfectly shaped and every curve ever so slightly accentuated, revealing her unrepressed sensuality. He noticed her legs first. Sun tanned. Smooth. Curvaceous. The calves were firm and rounded, falling to her slim ankles and perfectly shaped feet which were encased in high-heeled sandals, giving the effect that her legs continued for ever.

Philip's mouth felt dry. He swallowed unable to speak and she knew the effect she was having. She stood before him, one foot in front of the other, the weight of her body on one leg, the rounded thighs leaving their imprint on her black, tight skirt. A slit in the skirt revealed a few inches of her upper leg. His eyes automatically moved upwards. Her breasts were well rounded but in proportion to her body. He could see their firmness curving under the thin, low-necked top as they thrust themselves through the flimsy material, the nipples protruding.

'Mr Mason?' she purred, knowing exactly who he was.

Philip could hardly speak but nodded.

'Mr Jordan said you might need these,' she said, eyeing him with a look of arrogance mixed with indifference. Her voice was soft and silky with a trace of an American accent. She laid a pile of photographs on his desk and, without waiting for acknowledgement threw back her long, thick red hair which fell to her waist like molten copper. She turned to go.

'Thank you...thank you very much,' Philip said, hurriedly forcing himself to speak before she left. 'You must be Mike's

P.A.' half questioningly, one part of him wondering why he was bothering to talk. It was so out of character for him. He rarely looked at other woman but she intrigued him. He knew that he did not want her to leave just yet. She turned slowly and looked rather disdainfully down her small, pert nose.

'That's right.'

For a moment he imagined that she was going to smile.

'I heard someone new had started.' She said nothing but moved towards his desk. 'Is that a hint of an American accent I hear?' he smiled, desperately trying to make conversation.

'Maybe…' Her pink lips were moist, parting momentarily as she spoke. Her green eyes scrutinised him carefully. They were so penetrating and looked as though they could read his mind that a hot flush rose to his cheeks.

After a few moments, she edged herself onto the front of his desk and swung the top half of her body round to face him. Philip was taken by surprise. She now gave him the full effect of her smile and fixed him with her penetrating eyes. He felt powerless. Leaning forward, she loosened his crumpled tie and bent towards him. He could see the curve of her breasts as they dipped invitingly to her cleavage, smell the sweet warm fragrance of her body as she said seductively, 'You know you've been working too hard. You ought to take things easy for a while!'

She sprang from the desk and walked towards the door, her hips swinging knowing that his eyes had not left her. Quickly, she closed it behind her, leaving Philip puzzled, fighting with confused feelings of anticipation and yearning.

Once outside, she stood for a moment, smiling, inwardly congratulating herself. She had laid the bait and now all she had to do was wait until he wanted to eat. She did not mind how long it took but knew instinctively that it would not take long. Her plan was finally in motion.

'I've got to see you...it must be soon' Black's soft American drawl drifted down the phone making her tremble with excitement. She was silent for a moment.

'What can I tell Philip? You know how difficult it is for me to get away. What if he suspects?' the Blonde asked pleadingly not wanting to be confronted by her own feelings of guilt.

'Tell him what the hell you like!' Black was growing impatient. 'Does it matter if he finds out? 'Would you really be all that bothered...or would you rather we forget it?'

She was a little surprised at his attitude. He was callously pressurising her. His ego was sore.

'Awww! Come on, Honey. I've just gotta see you!' He felt he was begging and he had never had to do that before.

'All right,' she sighed 'I'll try to make it this weekend. Ring me Thursday and I'll know by then.'

She put her mobile back in her bag, noticing the perspiration on its cover as her excitement was rising at the prospect of seeing him again. It was no good fighting her feelings. She could not ignore the effect that Black had on her. She had been drawn into his web and was powerless to escape.

Philip came home shortly after that. He looked tired, his face set in its concrete stare. He was unwavering and threw a dark glance in her direction. She felt more remorseful than ever before. He put his briefcase on the floor and slumped heavily into one of the armchairs.

'Dinner's ready!,' she tried to sound cheerful, knowing that the evening ahead would be gloomy. 'Would you like me to dish it now?'

He turned cold, empty eyes to look at her.

'If you like.' He sounded disinterested and turned away. He did not speak throughout the meal but ate, careful to scrape the china plate with his knife and fork, a habit which he knew she hated. She wanted to scream 'Shut up! Stop making that noise!' but instead she supressed her anger and said nothing. It seemed that she was forever subduing her true feelings until she met Black and they had flown from her while she was with him in a continuing uninhibited stream. There was no turning back. Having tasted the sweetness of the wine, she was committed to finishing the bottle. So she became more determined as she surveyed Philip.

'I was thinking about visiting Leonie this weekend. She's very depressed and needs someone to talk to.'

The sound of her voice frightened her as much as the words she spoke. She waited tentatively for his reaction.

'If that's what you want.' His cold eyes rendered her motionless. A smile flickered over his lips. 'I'm sure I'll manage to entertain myself somehow!' An image of the redhead flashed through his muddled mind and he stood up from the table. 'How long is this going to continue?'

His question was like a knife being thrust into her stomach. He knew. She dropped her fork onto her almost untouched plate and stared into his eyes.

'I don't know what you mean…!'

'What I mean is…' and he began to spell it out in stilted language as though she were an idiot, 'How long are Leonie and Jeff going to live apart?'

She sank back inside herself with relief and almost over-eagerly answered his question.

'I suppose…as long as it takes Jeff to sort himself out.' She said nothing else as it occurred to her that she was moralising on Jeff's behaviour which was similar to her own. Clearing away the dinner plates, she tried not to think that not only was she letting Philip down but also Leonie when she needed her most.

It rained on Friday morning. The sky was grey and overcast with the first hint that summer was ending, the air holding a new crispness which crept in slowly, surprising the sun worshippers making their way to work with bare legs and sleeveless tops. The Blonde kissed Philip on the cheek. She didn't know why, perhaps to relieve her conscience or perhaps it was a ritual which had grown between them and she felt it would be sacrilege to dispense with. He brushed her away as quickly as possible this morning and turned to the door.

'Give Leonie my love. Perhaps I'll be able to go down with you one weekend soon.'

'Yes,' she replied softly as he closed the door.

She thought he had changed lately. He was mocking her. Perhaps he had given up all hope of her ever loving him completely which was the way he visualised their relationship. She did not know whether to feel pleased or sad at the prospect.

Philip's office lay at the back of the building overlooking a private courtyard where some of the occupants of the Centre spent their lunch hour sitting on the wooden benches beside the fountain, sunning themselves, their laughter floating up to the third floor where he sat in isolation, preferring his own company. He had a somewhat distinguished look. His once fair hair was now streaked with grey. His eyes were blue and intense while the broad jawline accentuated his firm mouth. He was neither a man's man nor a womaniser but a bit of a loner which added a certain mystery to his attraction.

Today the courtyard was deserted. The fountain still flowed while the rain dotted its surface making a constantly moving pattern which could almost mesmerise any onlooker. Philip stood alone, his face framed by the window, his eyes empty, looking down at the rain-soaked scene. He thought about the Blonde. She would be at Leonie's by now. He imagined her talking to Leonie, listening to Leonie, comforting Leonie, her ivory face animated in his mind. Her whole being was an elusive force which he despaired of ever grasping. He lit a cigarette and, after drawing on it heavily, stubbed it out in the ashtray.

Suddenly the door opened and he turned, startled by the sound, his daydreams disturbed. The redhead stood there, smiling, white even teeth glimmering like diamonds. He thought she looked beautiful and at that moment in time, he thought he had never seen anyone so beautiful. Feelings which lay dormant started to surface, pounding through his veins in an ever increasing beat. He sat down at his desk, momentarily embarrassed that she had caught him off guard.

'You're very elusive,' she said as she moved towards his desk. 'Don't you ever eat?' and without waiting for a reply, 'I thought I might see you in the canteen but who in their right mind eats there!' She laughed, tossing back her heavy mane. She was wearing a white, body-hugging cheesecloth top, buttoned at the front just to the point of respectability. She was well aware that the white complimented her tan, earned by careful organisation of summer days which added to her allure. A white skirt clung to her body, outlining the bare, bronzed legs. For an instant he was shocked at her presumptuous behaviour, but then he smiled finding the situation quite amusing and feeling flattered that she had sought him out.

'That's better,' she said,' You look almost human now!'

He began to like her impertinence. It was different, refreshing. He smiled again and found that he felt relaxed for the first time in months.

'Why did you want to see me?' he asked, intrigued to hear her answer.

'A number of reasons.' She stopped to think for a moment, giving him time to devour her appeal. 'The main one being that you've never noticed me until that day I came in here and I think the situation needs rectified! Girls always fall for a challenge, you know!' Her eyes, green as Jade, looked straight at him half seriously, half mockingly, waiting for his reaction. He blushed slightly. She was just a child on the inside, he thought, but definitely a woman in all other ways.

Phillip sat back in his chair and studied her. She could only be in her early twenties, he thought.

'How old are you?' he asked with a hint of the school master creeping into his voice.

She laughed at him.

'Old enough! Anyway, what gentleman asks a lady her age? Can I assume, then, that you are no gentleman?'

He smiled at her, feeling that he had been rightly reprimanded. Her face was now serious as she came round the edge of his desk; slowly, defiantly, with purpose in her eyes.

He knew what she wanted to happen. She came close to him. Her warm, sweet breath inviting him to kiss her but he turned away and swallowed hard.

'You like me, don't you?' Her voice was quiet and innocent.

'Yes, I like you.'

'Well...don't you want to kiss me?'

Her lips were eager and he responded willingly as she pulled him towards her. His first reaction had been to break away, tell her he was married, but her cool fingers entangled themselves in his hair, her hands working their way round his ears, neck and shoulders, awakening desire in his frustrated body. He responded automatically. He felt mellow and could feel the suppressed urge rising in him which the Blonde had failed to satisfy recently. Now she was furthest from his thoughts as he kissed the Redhead and she guided his hand to her firm breast. Suddenly, she broke loose from him and looked straight into his eyes. He was captivated. She started to unbutton the white pill shapes on her top. One...two...three...he counted as she ripped them apart...four...revealing the line her bikini had left on the tanned skin...five...six...and she pulled the soft material aside, revealing the silky soft breasts, full, firm and rounded. They were warm against his lips as he kissed them, her flesh yielding to his touch. His hands caressed them, his body bathing in the warmth and intimacy of hers. He was being pulled along by the strength of her charms, powerless against his own reasoning and now his lips wandered up to her neck.

'What...if someone...comes in?' he whispered.

'Don't worry...I locked the door when I came in,' she replied softly yet in an almost commanding voice. He did not even consider her foresight but slid his hand down the rounded curve of her body to her thigh, clothed in the soft material. His code of morals, ethics, reasoning were completely lost to him now as waves of unparalleled expectation gripped him as he pulled the flimsy material up and over her firm legs. She was warm and soft and willing and he thought of nothing but his own pleasure as he thrust himself between her thighs, relieving all the frustrations that the past months had heaped upon him. He felt the heat of her inner warmth penetrating him, soothing him as though it was running through his veins. She was never still, her hands moving over his body arousing feelings of which he was unaware.

In the dimly lit room, as the building filled with people returning from lunch their clothing speckled by the light rain, Philip shed his frustrations and experienced pleasures which had previously been merely fantasies.

# Five

'Leonie? It's me. How are you?'

'Just the same.' The voice sounded flat and emotionless. 'Nothing changes. Jeff is still in Norfolk refusing to accept his responsibility towards the kids and me. What can I do? There's nothing I can do.'

An awful silence followed.

'I'm sorry, Leonie. Give it more time. You'll see…things will work out. Jeff loves you. He'll come back eventually…just give him a little longer to work things out.' The Blonde surprised herself by the rational advice she was offering. 'I'm sorry to bother you now, I know you have a lot to deal with but I need your help. I've told Philip that I'm visiting you this weekend, which I really wish was happening, but I've got to see Black. It's so important that I see him this weekend otherwise I wouldn't ask.' She stopped, waiting for a response from Leonie. 'Leonie, are you still there?'

'Yes, I'm here. O.K. I'll cover for you. I only hope you know what you're doing!'

The Blonde wanted to tell Leonie that she felt she and Black were at a crucial stage in their relationship. That was why she had to see him this weekend but there seemed no point in burdening her with further information considering how low she sounded.

They said goodbye and the Blonde felt remorseful but an invisible force somewhere inside was pushing her onwards towards the unknown. Nothing could stop her now.

She drove her mini carefully into the car park and was surprised to see him already there. It gave her a thrill just to catch sight of him against his sleek car, the light glimmering along its bodywork, accentuating the curves, making them as glamorous as a woman's body. After helping her from her car, he crushed her in his iron-like grip, pressing his lips dominantly against hers. When she was with him, there seemed no other solution to her situation. It seemed so simple because all that mattered was being with him. He held her at arms' length and looked at her face, his blue eyes searching hers.

'How can you do this to me?' His voice was almost pleading. His lips moved slowly. She was unsure of his meaning and did not reply as he steered her towards his car with the words, 'We'll discuss this later. Let's get outta here.'

She felt it was all a game, his hurt pride blackmailing her into a situation over which she had no control. She thought that she was probably one of the few women who had questioned his motives and the situation fascinated him. She knew there would be other women in his life, and for the moment, she visualised his life stretching in front like a long road, peppered along the miles by different blondes; saw his dark hair slowly turning grey but the eyes still clear and intense blue, still able to attract any female he cared to look at. And she saw herself at the beginning of that road having been left behind. It became a bad dream so she closed her eyes and pushed it to the furthest recess of her mind.

Philip opened the door into an empty house full of memories of her. He poured himself a whisky and flopped down onto the settee. Drinking it in one, he ran his hand through his hair and listened to the silence. What had he done? How could he have done it? Had it only happened today…this morning? He asked himself a million questions but came up with only one answer. It was just one of those things which happen when defences are down and reason did not prevail. Every man was human and human weakness was in all of us, he told himself. Why should he be so different?

The day lay behind him, a blurred image, and self-reproach gripped him by the throat. How could he have had sex with that girl, someone he hardly knew? What the hell was wrong with him? But even as he chastised himself, a comforting sensation floated over his body, burying the guilt, reviving those same feelings which he had allowed to overflow a few hours earlier. He now knew why he had allowed himself to be seduced. He was like a hungry, scavenging animal, ready to devour any piece of meat which came his way. Damn her! She had done this to him! She had driven him away by denying his existence! The Blonde was to blame, not him.

The evening sunset seeped through the windows laying dark shadows over the room. Feeling the whisky take control of his body and iron out his reasoning, he poured himself another and drank it. Gripped by an all-consuming anger and hurt, he flung the empty glass against the fireplace. It shattered and hundreds of tiny pieces reflected the dying light of the day as they cascaded downwards to the floor. The noise wrenched Philip from his thoughts and highlighted his resolve. He jumped up unsteadily and reached for his jacket. He fumbled in the pockets, frantically searching, wondering if it had all been an illusion but then he found the familiar paper from his desk. Written in childlike handwriting was the information he sought.

'Andrea Winbech, 48 Cambridge Mansions' and a mobile number. Clasping the paper in his trembling hand, he punched in the number. Almost immediately, it was answered. It was as though she knew he would ring and for an instant, he hesitated and nearly ended the call.

'Hello', she said, her deep voice mellow and provocative, reminding him of that afternoon as she whispered softly in his ear, 'I wondered how long it would take you!' He could visualise her face, smiling seductively yet mocking him. She gave the impression that she knew exactly what he was thinking and feeling. 'How long will it take you to get over here?' she asked presumptuously.

'About fifteen minutes if I get a taxi,' he replied before he could stop himself.

'Fine. I'll keep it on ice for you!' and she laughed then hung up before he could say anything.

Andrea Winbech was 23 years old and lived in a sumptuous Victorian apartment block near the centre of the city. Her father had presented her with this present two years earlier on her 21st birthday. She had accepted it without grace minus much show of affection for him or his gift being of the opinion that it was her due. She had always been headstrong and neither cherished his affection for her nor denied it. Being his only child, Andrea held a special place in his heart, a heart that was made from stone like those which had built him into the cold-hearted property tycoon that he had become.

'Well, come in!' she ordered after opening the door to Philip. Immediately she turned from him into the large hallway, leaving him to make up his own mind. He stood for a moment, leaning against the doorway, tie undone, looking dishevelled as he watched her figure disappear into one of the many doors. He looked down at the floor and with great effort, manipulated his tired frame through the door, pushing it closed behind him. Soft music drifted from a room to the left and he entered to see her lounging on a large settee which could have held six. It was covered in a rich green material. It reminded him of her eyes and he wondered, in his stupefied state, if she had chosen it for that reason.

Looking at her now made him feel trapped. She motioned for him to sit beside her. He was not used to being ordered around. Then he noticed that she was wearing the flimsiest of dressing gowns. Like gossamer, it clung to the curves of her body, a shimmering of pink which kissed the outline of her figure as she moved. He could see her nipples lying quietly behind the silky screen like two pert untouchable shells newly plucked from their watery bed. He sat close to her. He wanted her now. The whisky had fired him with confidence. He parted the front of her dressing gown and slid his hand slowly inside her thigh. She did not object but responded to his touch so he moved further down to the warmth between her legs.

'So…' She smiled slowly, parting her dewy lips, her eyes almost hypnotising him. 'She's let you out tonight, has she?'

Philip was shaken and looked at her coldly.

'What do you mean?'

'Well, I hardly think your visit here would get your wife's seal of approval!' and she laughed moving her body closer to his.

'How do you know I'm married?' he asked nervously.

'You look married!' she laughed, 'Anyway, I've worked in the Centre long enough to know everybody!'

Fear gripped Philip but then he remembered how the Blonde treated him and he managed to dispel all guilt.

'She's gone away for the weekend,' he muttered. Andrea smiled inwardly. She visualised The Blonde and she knew exactly where she had gone.

'Why don't you leave her?' The words were as sharp as a knife being plunged into him. 'What have you got to stay for that you can't find right here with me?'

Philip did not reply. The dim lighting had turned shadows to black in the corners of the room where it looked like an empty, lifeless pit. Her hand stroked his hair and he felt the slightest pressure of it pulling him down, down, down as though he were falling. He could feel her firm breasts heaving softly, her heart beating quickly like a trapped bird. He kissed the rounded curves, emotions rising inside him, and again she guided the situation like the director of a play until their bodies were locked in an all-consuming passion, pressing into the sofa beneath them.

Her script was pure theatre, different every time. She had a repertoire which gave everything for that moment and, before it was over, she had already planned the next. She was a combination of sensual fantasy and sensitivity which no man could resist.

'How did you know I would phone?' he whispered quietly into her ear which lay in a clearing amongst the thick shining strands of red gold hair.

'I just knew you would! I have a way of getting what I want!' she chuckled almost grotesquely, musing that her plans were working out perfectly. The web had been spun and the prey caught.

'Why don't I take you out for dinner?' he asked. 'I know a nice little Italian not far from here.'

Unfortunately, Andrea also knew the little restaurant very well and could not risk being seen with Philip. Too many film and television people used it and might recognise them.

'Let's just stay here and eat,' she purred seductively and he agreed.

Philip stayed the whole weekend with Andrea and the longer he stayed, the less guilty he felt. He was beginning to imagine that he was in love with her and, to him, that made everything alright. The Blonde was now a mere ghostly image in his mind, a fleeting elusive shadow which drifted passed his eyes occasionally. He realised that he had never felt as relaxed as he now did with Andrea, and she in turn spent every moment ensuring that he would always want to come back to her but only when she wanted him.

Philip felt young again. The years seemed to shed themselves. He was the brash youth wallowing in her obvious hunger for him. She flamed his ego, restored his confidence and challenged his devotion to his wife.

Later, as they lay in bed satiated from making love, Andrea wrapped her sensuous body round his once again. Philip was sleeping but she could not. She tossed and turned but could not dispel an image of her mother, seven years before. Tall. Elegant. Cold. She stood before Andrea dressed immaculately in the latest Paris fashions, looking like the model she once was. Daddy stood quietly in the background. She was angry.

'You realise you can't keep this baby? It's out of the question!' she said in a clipped tone, 'The press would have a Field Day! You've got your father's reputation to think of.'

Daddy tried to intervene.

'Don't be too harsh on her, Marianne. She's just a kid herself.'

But Marianne was not prepared to listen to her husband.

'You'll have to get rid of it!'

Andrea had no choice. She was too young to argue so she had done as she was told. She now lay staring into the darkness while tears rolled down her cheeks and stained the pillow.

# Six

Leonie looked out of the French windows to the desolate, windswept garden. Rain stained the glass while fallen leaves were whipped against the window, halting for a second suspended in mid-air, then dropping to the paving stones below before being blown in another direction. It seemed that everything around her was dying. The summer. The trees. The flowers. Part of her had already died.

She turned from the gloomy scene and busied herself with preparing lunch. Weekends were the worst part, she thought, because Jeff and she had always made an effort to spend them together, devoting their time and energies to the children, after the business of the week had been completed.

Weekends with Jeff now came flooding back to her like the ever-changing pages of a picture book. Weekends at the cottage in Norfolk, running with the dog along the beach at Lowestoft. All of them running, laughing and playing together as a family. She remembered Jeff putting his arm round her shoulders, sheltering her from the wind as it whipped off the North Sea, biting into their faces and bodies while the children ran ahead with the dog. There were visits to Norwich with special treats, picnics on the way, cosy evenings with just the two of them curled up in front of the fire, secure in the knowledge that the children were asleep. These days were now history. Nothing could retrieve them. He was all she had ever wanted but now he had broken their bond.

She hated cooking now. There seemed no point. The children were too young to appreciate her efforts and no joy gained in performing the task. Saturdays and Sundays became an endless penitence as they reared their ugly heads with regularity. What had she done to deserve this? She had been a good wife and mother to their children. She could not really be blamed if she had lost some of the vivacity she had when they first met. She had always presumed that was how things were in life. People met, fell in love, married, had children then grew old together, contented with their lot. She had never imagined that there were still games to be played and had scoffed at articles in Women's Magazines such as 'How To Keep Your Man'. They belonged to another world but not to hers and she found it inconceivable that women, other faceless women, might go to such lengths to ensure a faithful husband. Now she wondered was it possible that she had been closeted in a vacuum shielded from the real ugliness of the outside world.

Suddenly she heard a crack and looked down to see the egg she was holding oozing out of her clenched fist, dripping over the work surface and down to the floor in a gooey expanding mass. Leonie did not realise how much anger was inside her.

'Christ!' she shouted, slamming her fist down and crushing the remainder of the shell. She hated Jeff. He had just left her to pick up the pieces of what was left of their life, left her to get on with it. He had waltzed out thinking only of himself not caring that it was exhausting looking after children on your own.

'Mummy, I'm hungry. When can we have lunch?'

It was the older child, a boy of five who stood in front of her, eyes large and pleading, reminding her of Jeff. His face plagued her every moment of the day. Perhaps his smile caught for an instant in time reminded her of Jeff's photos when he was a child or could it have been his eyes, screwed up against the light which reflected images of Jeff when she least expected it. Her son was there as a monument to their life before. She would never be able to escape the reminder. She tried to calm herself and sound normal.

'Just a moment, darling. Lunch won't be long.'

Assured by this, he ran off to the next room from where she could hear shrieks of laughter as he played with his younger sister. The separation from Jeff seemed to have had little effect on them both but he had lived on the perimeter of their lives, working during the days and seeing little of them in the evenings. It had been a gradual change since he began the affair and more and more he stayed overnight in London. His excuses drifted back to her, 'Got a rush job on, darling. Afraid I won't make it home tonight. Give the kids a kiss from me.'

His voice was deep and mellow. She could hear it now and she believed him because there was no reason to disbelieve him so she had dutifully kissed the children and waited. He had lied to her. How could he do that?

The only difference now was that she knew he would not be back tomorrow evening or the next and it was this which disturbed her. Her life was like a ship whose anchor had been severed and it was drifting out to sea. Unknown waters. No safe haven. Dark despair.

She searched in every drawer until she found them. They were small, white pills which the doctor had prescribed. She had never believed that pills helped and had put them away to be forgotten but, at the moment, she desperately needed something.

'You've had a terrible shock, Leonie. You may not realise how much this has affected you but it will manifest itself, given time. These will help ease the situation somewhat,' her doctor had said sympathetically.

She swallowed two, feeling the tiny pills slither over her throat and mingle with the water as they made their way through her body. Later, she prepared lunch as best she could, serving the children in a robot-like manner as they sat and chatted together, oblivious of her presence.

The rest of the day passed so slowly, every minute like an hour until bath time finally arrived. In fact she bathed them earlier than usual as time was dragging and she attempted to hurry it on. Safely tucked in bed, she kissed their soft, sweet cheeks, the scent of soap wafting from them, and they, in their innocence, kissed her back, the older whispering 'sweet dreams', a traditional game between them to which she would reply 'God Bless' and switch off the lights. Tonight, however, she returned to their beds and looked in turn at the angelic faces lit by moonlight, eyes closed now, a pink flush from the warm duvet kissing their cheeks, their breathing barely audible. She bent down and kissed them once again, painting their features on her memory, marvelling at their beauty and whispered softly to herself 'God forgive me.'

Alone again in the empty downstairs, she fumbled with the tiny pill bottle and pushed it deep into the pocket of her apron. Wandering around in a daze, she checked all the electrical appliances and saw that everything was safe to her satisfaction. No harm must come to the children through her carelessness.

Once again she made her way to the lounge. It felt cold and unlived in and she thought that was the way it should feel as there was no longer a family there. She poured herself a large brandy and sat down on the sofa. The little pill bottle pressed into her body from the depths of her pocket and she pulled it out, holding it in her hand, turning it round, examining the contents as though seeing them for the first time.

The brandy was making her feel sleepy and so she hurriedly poured herself another, even larger, glass and started to swallow the pills. Just a few at first then more as she crammed them into her mouth, hastening their progress with large gulps of the copper liquid and soon the pill bottle lay empty as her side. She allowed herself to think about Jeff for just a moment. It hurt too much. She thought about the other woman and cursed her.

'May she rot in Hell!'

Tears stung her eyes as she thought of the children sleeping upstairs. Her one ambition in life had been to see them grow, watch them through each stage and marvel at their achievements. She was denying herself this and tears rolled down her face, stinging her skin. There was no other way.

'Please God, keep them safe,' she whispered before a black blanket of oblivion enshrouded her, leaving Leonie with the peace she sought.

# Seven

A tractor moved methodically over the upturned field like some insane monster, back and forth from each end of the brown expanse leaving neat furrowed lines behind. Fresh earth, a darker, moister brown was regurgitated to the surface by the long teeth of the machine eating into the crust of the land as the plough moved on. Gulls flew behind looking for food, dancing back and forth to a frenzied beat. They wailed and squawked above the tractor engine. Nothing else moved against the steel blue sky, tinted with grey as dusk enveloped the early September night. A car engine could be heard in the distance, slowly eating into the silence as it advanced into the scene.

The tractor driver turned momentarily to his fellow workers and nodded in the direction of the car.

'It's them again!' he shouted above the tractor's loud, gravely drone. 'They're back again!' He grinned and his white teeth added an unexpected touch of illumination to his weather beaten face which lay in creases like well-worn leather. 'They ain't been 'ere for a while, eh?' But it's the same one 'e got with 'im, that blonde one!'

They turned from looking at the car as it sped past them towards the village, the tractor driver shaking his head in disbelief and smiling.

Black turned to the Blonde as he brought the car to a halt outside the old hotel.

'Smile, Honey! It can't be as bad as that!'

She found it difficult to feel happy, plagued by thoughts that she should really be with her sister. She was also wearying of the same routine with Black. She felt he was keeping her in the background, an awful secret.

He turned her chin towards him and kissed her gently on the lips then drew back from her, his blue eyes penetrating hers. She searched them for some meaning but could find none.

'Come on. Let's go in!' he urged, getting out of the car, his feet crunching on the gravel as he opened her door.

The hotel had not changed in appearance since their first visit that summer. Paint still flaked on the outside walls. If anything, the summer sun had given it warmth which it did not possess. Now the September evening showed it in its true light—cold and uninviting, emphasising the unspoken words which lay like a screen between them. Many times they had driven the same road and said the same things but today was different. She sensed the atmosphere had changed. Their relationship had reached a defining moment.

'Why must we come here?' she asked, the question escaping her lips like the desperate wail of a wounded animal.

'You know why, Kitten,' he replied, his arm protectively round her shoulder, 'Anywhere else and I'd be recognised, wouldn't I?' and without waiting for a response, kissed her ear which nestled amongst her golden hair. 'We want some peace, don't we?'

They walked up the well-worn steps, their arms entwined. She noticed that the room had not changed much. Only the curtains had been replaced with a much thicker pair to keep out the cooling autumn wind. Gone were the thin cotton prints of the summer months, another sign that winter was about to descend leaving her despondent.

'I've got something to tell you and also something to ask!' Black said, excitedly. He sat down beside her on the bed. She smiled and draped her slim arms round his neck.

'Alright,' she whispered, kissing his mouth with small, delicate kisses, 'Tell me the first bit.'

His answer was unexpected.

'I'm going back to the States!'

She stopped kissing him. Her hands lay motionless on his shoulders. She was shocked. Fear overcame her and the colour drained from her face.

'Going back...? For how long...? When?'

Her questions came all together, not one having priority over the rest, as she trembled underneath her flimsy sweater.

'Quite soon and for quite a while! A new movie has come up. I like the script and it's too good a chance to turn down!'

She turned away from him, trying desperately to calm herself. She tried not to panic. Why hadn't she expected that this time would come sooner or later. Had she imagined that things would stay the same or had she not wanted to imagine them differently?

'Hey, look at me!' Black coaxed her, 'You haven't asked me what I have to ask you yet!'

He pulled her towards him and held her in his arms. He looked wonderful. Fresh. Irresistible and she felt dread rise inside.

'What were you going to ask me?' she whispered nervously.

'I'm going to ask you if you'll come with me!'

She heard the words which inspired mixed emotions. He was wanting her to go with him, to be with him but there were still doubts in her mind, pulling her back. She put her arms round his warm body and kissed him.

'You'll come then?' he asked eagerly.

'Well…of course I want to…but…' she faltered.

'Gee, but what?' he demanded and turned away to hide his disappointment. 'Hell, what is there to think about? You either love me and want to be with me or you love him and want to stay.' He stood up, his brow furrowed, his eyes darkening with annoyance. His ego was bruised. 'You just can't have both of us!' He had never mentioned 'love' before.

'Black,' she stretched out her hand to him, 'you know how I feel about you but it's not as simple as that!' She felt she was placating the child in him. 'You just can't be married to someone for years and write it off in a day!'

'Write it off in a day?' he growled, kneeling on the bed, his face close to hers. 'Is that how you think of the last few months? Well, Hell, if I'd known, Baby, I might not have stuck around for so long!'

He rose from the bed and turned to the window. Dusk was falling, dark and dense. The field outside was a mass of grey, shapeless shadows. He saw her reflection in the window and her words cut into him.

'Do you really love me, Black?'

He looked like a lost child and did not turn around.

'Sure I love you...now, at this moment in time. If love is wanting to be with you and nobody else, then I love you now.' He paused. 'Who knows how I'll feel tomorrow or the next day or the day after that!'

He wanted to punish her, to make her feel as bad as he felt now. It was what she had expected to hear and yet dreaded hearing him utter the words as she drifted once again into her own insecurity. He turned and knelt in front of her, almost pleading, while he held her hands firmly in his.

'But I love you now! That's what matters! Now we can be together. Isn't it just amazing? I can show you places, take you to these places, show you off! We won't need to stay in dumps like this. We'll be official! We'll be free! Can't you see how it will be for us?'

She could see clearly. She could imagine not having to feel guilty about meeting, being able to completely relax and enjoy each other and share his fame instead of being relegated to the background. It would be as she always imagined it would be.

'I still need time, Black...just a little time.'

'O.k.' He stood up and ran his fingers through his hair, 'O.K. Take some time but don't make it too long.'

She could tell that his pride was hurt but she wondered if he was capable of deeper feelings which she could trust.

They made love after dark when the light of the moon seeped through the sides of the thick curtains where they failed to cover the window completely. He still excited her. They still had passion but the relationship had moved on. Some enthusiasm had gone and it had been stripped of its fantasy quality to expose the reality underneath. Was the reality what she wanted or was she in love with a dream? She lay awake for some time pondering this in her mind, looking at the moonlight creeping over the ceiling. Some moments she was wildly excited at the prospect of going to America with Black then panic would creep in at the thought of leaving her home and familiar surroundings.

It was late Sunday evening when the Blonde parked her car on the drive. She had arrived later than anticipated but it had taken time and patience to restore Black's injured ego. The street lighting cast a yellow light over the area as she locked the car and prepared herself mentally for Philip's questions about her weekend with Leonie. She felt quite pleased with herself. She felt at peace with Black and confident that she could deal with Philip. Now that Black had asked her to go to the States, it didn't really matter what Philip thought. Black loved her.

Stealthily, she placed her key in the lock trying not to make a noise and hoping to creep to her bedroom to gather herself together before meeting Philip. She could tell that he hadn't gone to bed as the lounge lights were shining through the blinds. Gently, she pushed open the front door and almost immediately a shadow fell over her. Philip was standing in front of her. His face looked peculiar, contorted and his eyes were glazed.

'Philip…' she started. He immediately advanced towards her.

'Where the hell have you been?' he shouted then slapped her face with his hand. It was a sharp, short, icy slap which stunned her momentarily then immediately turned to searing heat. Every tooth in her mouth seemed to be hurting. Her trembling hand moved instinctively to her mouth and she saw the moist, red blood trickling between her fingers. Her lips felt as though they were detached from her body. 'Jesus, I'm sorry! I shouldn't have hit you!' he said and made his way to the bathroom to get a cold cloth which he handed to her. 'But I ought to fucking kill you!'

He grabbed her by the shoulders as she held the cloth to her mouth. She had never seen him like this before. She tried to speak but the words would not come. He shook her until she thought her head would fall off. Then he pushed her away and sat on the two bottom stairs, holding his head in his hands. Her head ached and her eyes stung. She started to weep uncontrollably.

'Christ knows where you've been while your sister is lying half dead!'

She looked at him with disbelief.

'Leonie...?' she whispered feeling the thickness of her lip.

'Yes, Leonie!' he shouted as he stood up. He pushed an accusing finger into her body making her lurch against the door. 'Where were you when she needed you? Certainly not where you said you would be!'

He turned away giving her a contemptuous look.

'Philip!' she cried, her hand outstretched to him. 'Philip!' She wept. 'What happened? Tell me what happened!' She screamed hysterically. By this time, he was in the lounge and she followed him, her legs barely able to support her as she flopped onto a sofa.

'I'll tell you what happened,' he spat, 'She was only so depressed that she downed all the doctor's pills and a bottle of brandy last night. The weekends are so long, you see, when you haven't a husband and have children to cope with!' He was threateningly close to her face now and she tried to back away, sinking further into the settee. 'Of course if you have a sister…' He continued sarcastically, 'who visits you at weekends, it helps take some of the strain after spending all week with no one to speak to!' He turned and made his way to the drinks cabinet, poured himself a large whisky and took a huge gulp while the Blonde, still sobbing, dabbed her lip with a fresh tissue. He turned towards her and stood menacingly in front of her. 'Then again, if that sister happens to be you, you have to cover for her while she goes off enjoying herself, indulging in some seedy little affair and leaving you to die!'

He leaned into her face to deliver the last words and she could stand it no longer.

'Shut up! Shut up!' she shouted. 'Stop it, please! Where is she?'

'She's in hospital! Luckily she's not in the morgue. You'll be saved that thanks to a neighbour who saw the light on late and became suspicious. Got her just in time!'

'Is she going to be all right?' she asked pathetically.

'I hope so,' he said flatly.

The blonde buried her head in her hands, realising the enormity of what she had done and how selfish she had been. Devastation overpowered her and she rocked back and forwards as she asked herself repeatedly, 'What have I done? What have I done?'

She sat this way for some time until she was conscious only of the noises emanating from herself into the silence of the room. Philip sat quietly looking at her calculatingly watching her torment but no matter how much he tried to hate her, he could only feel compassion. She watched him through clouded eyes as he moved through the room. He knew now. Everything had changed. Her life was a mess.

'Here,' he said softly averting his eyes from hers and handing her a fresh bowl of warm water. 'You'd better clean that cut then I'll drive you down to the sea. Leonie's kids will need you now.' She looked at him like a frightened animal caught in a trap but he quickly turned away. There was a barrier between them which both now acknowledged. 'Put some things in a bag and we'll go,' he ordered.

It was a long drive. The Blonde felt her head aching, an ominous pulsating behind her eyes. Philip drove in silence, his face set in a firm, determined line. The road stretched endlessly ahead, straight carriageways cutting into the countryside in all their artificiality. Trees loomed out of the darkness, like ghostly statues, at irregular intervals on the side of the road. She shivered and pulled her coat closer to her body, trying to generate some heat into her shocked flesh. Car headlights, like dual sets of enormous animal eyes, drifted towards them in ever increasing numbers. She felt sick from the monotonous motion of the car. Claustrophobia over powered her and a sinking feeling in her gut engulfed her.

Eventually, Philip turned off the motorway and they followed narrow roads lined by hedgerow. No cars passed them in the darkness, only Philip's headlights caught, for a fleeting instant, a nocturnal animal as it scampered for safety. After some time he slowed down and stopped outside a large, imposing building, the lights of which seemed curiously dimmed, casting a sombre glow over the car.

'This is the hospital,' he said, flatly.

She looked puzzled, her heart thumping.

'But…' She muttered 'It's late…'

She couldn't see Leonie now! What would she say? Words would never express how she felt inside.

'The very least you can do is enquire about her!' Philip said as he heaved himself from the driver's seat. She sat panic stricken while he opened her door. 'Come on,' he ordered, no hint of compassions in his eyes or in his tone. He turned ahead of her as she searched for her handbag, tentatively stepping out of the car, wondering if her legs would take the weight of her guilt ridden body.

There was a strong smell of disinfectant as they entered. She hated hospitals and remembered being left in one as a very small child, wondering why her mother and sister were allowed to go home when she had to stay. She could see their faces now through the window of her hospital ward. They were waving goodbye to her. She hated the clinical atmosphere and her hatred was born of fear.

Philip was whispering to the man behind the desk at Reception. Snippets of conversation floated through the silence to her ears. 'Admitted yesterday evening…'

Was it really only yesterday? 'Driven from London… her sister… she's in Ward 3' The man listened attentively then pointed towards the stairs.

They tiptoed together along corridors, passing wards bathed in slumber and whiteness. The Blonde fought against approaching waves of nausea as they arrived at the ward entrance. A nurse approached them and looked accusingly at Philip. Still whispering, he explained their late arrival. The Blonde did not listen. Her thoughts were elsewhere then the nurse spoke more loudly.

'She's asleep and is comfortable. I'm afraid there is absolutely no possibility of seeing her tonight. Tomorrow, perhaps tomorrow.' And she turned, her black stockings catching the glow from the light on her table as she disappeared into the gloom where motionless figures lay sleeping, their melodious breathing sometimes floating on the air to where she and Philip stood. He turned to her.

'Jeff's back at the house. I'll drop you there then I must get back to London.'

She had an urge to put her arms round him, beg him to stay but hesitated and the moment passed. They moved off in silence.

Jeff opened the door and the light from the hall flooded the pathway with a warm brilliance which penetrated the dark night.

Philip drove off with only a cursory glance in her direction and she felt abandoned.

'I'm so glad you're here,' Jeff said, kissing her icy cheek, 'I could never have managed the kids on my own.' He looked gaunt and haggard, thin and unkempt. There was a lifelessness in his eyes which she had never seen before. 'I've prepared the spare room for you. You should be quite comfortable in there.' He scrutinised her face for a moment. There was a brotherly warmth about him which made her relax a little and feel better.

'What happened to your lip?' he asked with concern. Her fingers automatically moved to her mouth and she could feel the swelling. In all the confusion of the night, she had completely forgotten about it.

'Nothing,' she quickly replied, her eyes betraying her. 'Do you mind if I go straight to bed, Jeff? It's been a long day.'

'Oh, no, of course not! How selfish of me. It's just so nice to see you again—it's been a while. But we can talk in the morning.'

He carried her case up to the spare room. 'Morning' the Blonde thought, when I shall have to deal with the reality of what I've done.

# Eight

She did not sleep well. Snippets of nightmares dissolved in her mind then recurred. Over and over again, she kicked out in her distress, removing the duvet then wakening herself because of the cold. Sometimes she woke and wondered where she was, unable to recognise her surroundings. About dawn, she finally fell into a deep sleep and was able to temporarily close out all thoughts.

She was awakened by the sensation of someone being in the room. She could hear faint breathing close to her. Opening her eyes quickly, she saw a small figure examining her closely.

'What have you done to your mouth?' her nephew asked, his gaze never moving from her face. She remembered and could tell it was still swollen as a pulsating throb ate into the stillness of her body. She said nothing but ruffled his hair and attempted a smile. Fortunately, Jeff called him downstairs. She turned over and stretched. Visions of the previous day hit her hard. Phillip. Leonie. Black. They all had a piece of her conscience and she wondered how she could face the future.

Presently, she heard noises from the kitchen and the child came back.

'Daddy's making breakfast 'cos mummy's in hospital and I have to go to school and Melanie has to go to nursery.' He stood at the side of her bed, smiling, exposing a missing tooth, blonde curls falling over his freckled forehead. He looked at her with innocent eyes. 'Are you going to stay with us?'

He looked so much like Jeff. There was little of Leonie about him. Leonie…the thought made her feel so remorseful. She struggled up and pushed her legs out of the bed.

'Of course I will. I'll stay until mummy comes back.'

'Oh, good!' he shrieked with delight and ran out of the room. She wrapped her pink dressing gown around her and flushed as she looked at the wrap remembering its recent associations in her life. Black's arms around her when she was wearing it, Black touching her underneath it. It all seemed dishonest now and she ripped it from her body, throwing it aside. A cardigan covered her as she made her way to the bathroom.

Jeff stood hunched over the sink when she came downstairs. He didn't hear her come in and seemed to be lost in thought.

'Are you alright?' she asked.

He turned quickly.

'Sorry, I was miles away!' He gave her a hug and she noticed that his eyes were red rimmed and bleary. 'I've just dropped the kids at school…it's hit me …what I've been missing.' He suddenly remembered that she hadn't had any breakfast or even a drink. 'Look, I'm sorry…I'm forgetting you. I'm so glad you're here. What would you like to eat?'

'Nothing, thanks. Just coffee, please.'

He poured them both a coffee and they sat at the table. He had aged a great deal. Grey flecked his hair and his face bore an unhealthy hue. She thought he looked ill. He was much thinner than she remembered. Being tall, the loss of weight seemed to accentuate his gangling limbs making his movements look awkward.

'The last few months have been hell and it's taken something like this… I mean, Leonie doing…what she did, to bring me back to my senses.' He stirred sugar into his coffee making the spoon repeatedly hit the sides of the cup, the noise irritating her delicate state. 'I've been such a bloody fool, thinking of myself all the time. It's all my fault… all my stupid fault. How could I be such an idiot? God knows what I was thinking of.' He seemed to be speaking to himself, almost unaware that she was there. 'I gave all this up. Leonie, the kids, the house…everything I've spent my life working for. I left everything for a woman half my age. How could I be so blind?' He rubbed his eyes and she could tell there were tears there. He sighed. 'We'll have this then go to the hospital if that's alright?'

She nodded.

'Aren't you going to eat anything, Jeff?' she asked concerned.

'No! Don't have the stomach for it. I feel so responsible for what Leonie has done. What if she had died? You see, I gave her little support through all this. I just left. At the time, I couldn't face it any other way. I felt so desolate.' His face wrinkled up, reliving the agonising experience. He obviously wanted to talk about it so the Blonde let him continue. 'When she left me…the girl, that is… I felt that everything had ended for me. She was so vibrant, so young, so beautiful.' As he visualised her, his eyes took on a new vibrancy. He was alone with her in his mind. 'She was completely different from

Leonie. Leonie only wanted to talk about the children and things connected with the house which was natural, I suppose… but…I resented it because she didn't seem to have time for me. She couldn't switch off and join in the outside world which was my world.' He hesitated and looked beyond her. The Blonde began to be annoyed on Leonie's behalf. She was her sister and she felt her betrayal. 'Looking back now, I can see how idiotic I was to feel that way. I should have tried to understand but men don't think the same way about these things as women do. After a hard working day, I needed some distraction and all Leonie seemed to be offering was a noose round my neck.' The Blonde was irritated now. She wanted to scream at him. She wanted to tell him that he was a selfish bastard but she stopped herself. She thought about Leonie missing him so much and then she thought that she was not in a position to criticise him. She let him indulge himself. 'Then she came along. I was flattered that she found me attractive. She was like a breath of fresh air, so beautiful and attractive. She gave me back a bit of my youth.' The Blonde scowled at him. She did not like what she was hearing and was discovering another side to the Jeff she knew. The adage, 'no fool like an old fool' came to mind. He did not notice her expression, so wrapped in his own thoughts. 'I was completely unaware of her at first, not looking for anything or anyone…but somehow…she crept into my life and was always there. Anywhere I went, she was there looking wonderful. I suppose it was inevitable what happened really. I couldn't ignore her. I was so weak, I couldn't stop it. I was absolutely hooked. I started behaving completely out of character, was hell to live with and poor Leonie could tell there was something up. Eventually, I told her because by that time I wanted to leave and marry the girl. Huh!' He flung back his head and laughed manically. He was becoming more agitated. 'Divorce Leonie and marry her! What was I thinking of but then she seemed quite keen. She had inflated my ego so much by then that I thought it might be possible and that it could work. I moved out and moved in with her but, after a few weeks, she told me there was someone else in her life, someone from a while ago who had come back into it and she had never stopped loving him. I was hurt. I felt I couldn't live without her and buried myself at the cottage in Norfolk. It took me ages to come to terms with the fact that she had left me and was never coming back. I never gave a thought to what I had done to Leonie.' He let out an anguished wail and cupped his head in his hands. 'As time passed...I began to realise what I had done to her but I was not big enough to admit it and ask her to take me back...not after all that had happened.' He began to sob and cradled his coffee cup in his hands. The Blonde had never seen a man cry.

'Don't!' she scolded as she rose from the table. 'Don't go on about it! I've heard enough!'

He looked startled.

'I'm sorry', he said slowly 'I shouldn't be unburdening myself to my wife's sister.'

'It's not advisable,' she said, 'but I understand how you feel.'

'You do? How can you?' he croaked.

'Because I should have been here. She needed me but I was so involved in my own selfishness that I put myself before her!' It was painful for her to explain. She might as well just say it. 'I've been having an affair and Leonie was my excuse...alibi...call it what you like.' Jeff's eyes were expressionless and there was a long silence. Then the blonde continued, 'I told Philip I was visiting Leonie this weekend but I was with him! How stupid! I could see the state Leonie was in the last time I saw her yet I ignored it…conveniently.'

Jeff stood up and refilled their coffee mugs. He sighed a long wavering sigh and sat down, putting his hand on top of hers and patted it reassuringly.

'Look,' he said flatly, 'Don't blame yourself. You mustn't. If it hadn't been for my actions, Leonie wouldn't have done this.' It did little to alleviate the shame she felt. 'And the lip?' he asked. 'How did that happen?'

Instinctively her hand reached up to her mouth. It was still slightly swollen but the throbbing had subsided.

'Philip. He's never hit me before. I suppose that hurt more than the actual physical pain…that our relationship had finally sunk so low but I can understand his reasons.'

'And this man? Are you going to continue this affair?'

'I don't know. He's asked me to go to America with him but I'm so confused. I can't make a decision about anything at the moment.'

'What about Philip?'

She sipped her coffee and thought for a second.

'Naturally, if it wasn't for Philip I'd go tomorrow but I can hardly deny his existence or the years we've spent together. I hardly know how I managed to get myself into this mess in the first place.' She stopped for an instant and rubbed her eyes. 'Since we're being so honest, it was probably boredom…the Seven Year Itch or something like that.'

Jeff looked at his watch and cleared away the coffee cups.

'Philip's a great guy but I hope it all works out for you. You must have your reasons just as I had mine. I wouldn't for a minute try to advise you or think I had the right to do so but I wouldn't like you to go through what I've gone through.'

'It's too late now!' She shrugged her shoulders.

The day was beautiful although there was a crispness in the atmosphere. The sun shone giving the world a fresh glow. Great streaks of sunlight cut into the car interior as Jeff drove to the hospital. The Blonde screwed up her eyes against the light and the silence between them allowed her to recall the events of the previous evening when Philip had driven her to the hospital. A cold fear possessed her as she thought of him.

Sunlight flooded the ward casting shadows. One lay over Leonie. There was a somnolent atmosphere all around. Her eyes were closed, her face holding a pallor closer to death than life. The Blonde shuddered. Her sister was almost unrecognisable. Drips were attached to her arm and different bottles and contraptions surrounded her bed.

Jeff and the Blonde stood side by side. He took Leonie's pale, cold hand in his. It seemed so small yet a neat hand with nails which were tiny and pink like the little shells they used to search for on the beach at Lowestoft.

A nurse approached the bedside and checked a monitor.

'Only five minutes, please. I don't think she'll be able to take more than that…totally exhausted. You can come back later.' And she moved off in a surge of starched officialdom.

Leonie slowly opened her eyes and tried to focus. She blinked against the light and turned her head slightly. She looked old. Grey showing through her hair was accentuated now and deep black circles ringed her eyes which did not seem to have recognition. She looked at them both for several minutes then a slight smile crossed her face, brightening the faded eyes.

'Jeff,' she whispered then tears came as she remembered. She pushed his hand away and looked beyond him to where the Blonde stood. Leonie stretched out her thin arms towards her sister and the Blonde clasped their coldness in the warmth of her own.

'Leonie, thank God you're OK! I'm so sorry!'

The tears somersaulted down her face, stinging her skin and nipping her cracked lip. A glazed look came over Leonie as though she had no comprehension of what her sister was saying.

'Now I think you've had your five minutes,' the nurse returned, 'She's had enough for today!' and she pulled the screen round Leonie's bed separating them from her. 'I'll be back in two minutes, Leonie, to check your BP,' and she ushered them to the door of the ward while Jeff pleaded, 'Can't I just have a little longer with my wife?'

'No, sorry, it's out of the question. You know she's been in a bad way...got to take things easy...she's not out of the woods yet!'

And she left them to make their way out of the hospital, across the grass which surrounded the building and back to the car. The Blonde felt so alone and for a moment, wished that Philip were with her but it was a habit rather than want.

'My God, that was hell!' Jeff slumped into the driver's seat. 'Seeing Leonie so frail and vulnerable...' His voice drifted into the silence as he started the car and they moved off. The evening came quickly and with it the business of making dinner, bathing the children and putting them to bed.

'Do you know what I made at school today?' Timothy sat on her knee, his sweet, melodious voice overflowing with pleasure. They sat in front of a large wood burner, the glow of the flames giving an added brilliance to his animated face. 'We made cakes and then we ate them! I had some left to bring home but Johnny dropped the plate and Frances stood on them!' He held back his head and laughed revealing his small even teeth with the gap in the middle. She smiled at him. 'Daddy says we can make some at the weekend. Will you help?'

He turned an enquiring face towards her. He was freshly washed and smelt of soap.

'Of course I shall,' she replied feeling slightly cornered knowing that she would still be needed at the weekend. 'Weekends were the worst time' she remembered Leonie's words. She had to stay.

Since the visit to the hospital, Jeff had found renewed energies. He had busied himself cooking the meal, bathing the children and had even lit the wood burner as approaching winter announced her presence. The Blonde had felt superfluous in the midst of these activities and stood on the side lines watching, only helping if asked. It seemed as though she was intruding on something very personal.

After putting the children to bed, Jeff joined her next to the fire. He organised more logs into the burner and she watched the sparks fly as he launched them into the inferno and closed the door.

'I feel marvellous,' he said sitting back on the sofa, 'It's as though it's all been a nightmare and I've wakened up to find that it's all right. We're going to manage, Leonie and I, and I'll make it up to her somehow but the main thing is that she gets better and is willing to give me a second chance.' He paused to gather his thoughts. 'I really do realise what I've missed but I suppose it has to take something like this to happen before I could appreciate it to the full.' The Blonde thought about Leonie and their last conversation where she had missed him so much yet felt so bitter that he had just left without a backward glance. 'I have great plans for us. First of all, I want to sort out a few things which I should have done before…like getting the kitchen decorated before Leonie comes home and buy those new units she's been longing for!' He looked into the distance imagining it then he turned to her. 'I know it seems a bit tame, as though I'm trying to buy back her affection or salve my conscience but it's a start, isn't it?' He looked at her questioningly.

'Of course it is,' she said quietly, 'Leonie missed you so much. The bottom fell out of her world when you left.'

He gave her a steady gaze and said nothing.

The doorbell rang and she could hear voices in the hall. Jeff was speaking to a neighbour who had offered to babysit while he and the Blonde visited Leonie in the early evening.

Leonie was propped up on a pillow still surrounded by drips, wires and machines. A different nurse was pouring her a glass of water when they arrived and she smiled.

'Oh, look, Leonie, you have some visitors. Isn't that nice! I'll just plump up those pillows and make you feel more comfortable.' And she busied herself punching the pillows, gently pulling Leonie into a sitting position. The Blonde moved forward and proffered the flowers she had brought. Leonie smiled slightly and the nurse took them away.' I'll find a vase for these.'

The Blonde sat down on a chair at the side of Leonie's bed and Jeff sat at the other side. He leaned over to kiss Leonie's cheek but she turned to the Blonde.

'I don't want you to blame yourself,' she said to her, 'I knew what I was doing.'

'I should have been there…' the Blonde started to speak but was interrupted by Jeff.

'It was all my fault! I should never have left like I did!'

Leonie did not look at him but stared steadily at the Blonde.

'What the fuck is he doing here?' I never want to see him again!' Her voice was hard and determined.

'But darling…' Jeff pleaded as she turned to him.

'Fuck! That's the word! You fucked her several times, didn't you! Get him out of here!' she screamed and the nurse came hurrying in.

'I think you'd better leave. She mustn't get upset.'

Jeff again tried to speak to her but the Blonde took his arm and ushered him out of the ward. They sat in the car in silence then he turned to her.

'I never thought she'd react like that, did you?' he asked.

The Blonde admired her sister's strength and resolve although her reaction had been unexpected. Leonie had survived and the experience had made her stronger.

'She's still hurting, 'she replied. 'It's still very raw. Give her time.'

He hunched over the steering wheel, never making a move to start the engine.

'What am I going to do?' he wailed, trembling, 'I don't feel like I belong now! All my plans have flown out of the window!'

He looked desperate and she tried to console him.

'Don't jump to conclusions too quickly. Maybe you should stay away from the hospital for a while. I'll visit her alone tomorrow. Let her recover first.'

He seemed to accept what she said. They drove home in silence until Jeff said, 'I've been too busy thinking about my own problems, I completely forgot about yours. I'm sorry. How do you feel…about things between Philip and you?' He sounded almost embarrassed.

'I don't know. So much has happened in such a short time.' Her voice droned just above the engine. 'I don't think things can ever be the same between us. He'll never forgive me…do I even want his forgiveness?'

Jeff and Philip had always been very close and she sensed that Jeff felt his agony.

'Why don't you give him a ring when we get back?'

Jeff was distraught after the babysitter left. He sat at the fire staring into space. All his plans seemed to have disintegrated. He seemed destroyed and the Blonde decided to give him space.

Later she rang the familiar number, imagining Philip sitting in their lounge, his brows furrowed, a newspaper stretched between his hands. She did not know what she would say to him. Perhaps just tell him that Leonie was recovering. She only wanted to hear his voice and she would feel secure again.

The telephone rang at the other end twice, six times. Any minute now he would answer and say 'Hello' she thought but it continued to ring. Perhaps he's in the bath she thought trying to console herself so she tried his mobile. No answer. A sickening twinge of isolation swept over her. Where had he gone? It was too late for him to be at the studio. It was completely unlike Philip. Normally he returned home at the usual time, his pleasures in life being few and work taking priority. He seldom drank apart from social occasions and she knew there was nowhere he was likely to go alone straight form work. She decided to try again later while thinking that perhaps she did not know her husband at all.

# Nine

Philip had arrived home from Leonie's in the early hours of Monday morning. The drive had exhausted him so he decided to have a long sleep. He would go to the studio later in the day. After all, there was no urgency about the current work and he had things on his mind. It would be impossible to concentrate.

He lay in the cold bed, turning one way and then the other, trying to find a comfortable position but the sleep which he so badly craved, evaded him. He decided not to fight it any longer and while he lay staring up at the ceiling, he started to think about the Blonde. He saw her eyes looking at him after he had hit her. They were like those of a wounded animal. He felt ashamed. He had never hit anyone before. He wasn't an aggressive person but something inside him had snapped.

He wondered where she had been and who she had been with and he envisioned this imaginary person with his wife, kissing her, holding her, touching her. And he saw himself, living his life, unaware of her unfaithfulness, completely oblivious to the fact that she could deceive him or that there could be someone else. He felt angry and hurt and foolish and wondered what could have brought them to this. Life was full of cruel twists. If Leonie had not tried to kill herself, perhaps he would never have known that the Blonde was being unfaithful.

He had seen it in her eyes the night he struck her. The guilt stared at him from the depths of her being, as though a curtain had been torn from a window revealing the view inside. She was a selfish cow. If only she had explained. Surely she owed him that much and yet she had insisted that there was no one else therefore no apparent reason for her coldness towards him. She was as changeable as the weather, a butterfly floating from one flower to the next.

He supposed she had always been rather unsettled, never satisfied with one state of affairs, constantly changing their situation. First, it had been flats, then clothes and finally cars. It was not that she was particularly materialistic but it seemed that her yearning for adventure and constant change needed to be satisfied. It had been exciting when he first met her and he became caught up in her enthusiasm. It had enriched his otherwise monotonous lifestyle but gradually he tired of it. His pleasures were simple and he sought simple solutions in his life. Somehow it was not enough for her.

Lying there, Philip became aware of the change in intensity of light behind the blind which covered the bedroom window. Slowly the dawn slithered round its edge and seeped into the room. He looked at the clock. Nearly 7am. His eyes reluctantly closed and he drifted into a deep sleep. He dreamt of a phone ringing but then the dream became reality and crept into his consciousness with its piercing insistent ring. He propped himself on one elbow and fumbled for his mobile. By now the sun was high in the sky casting an even pink glow over the bedroom as it shone through the red blind.

'Hello' he managed to mutter groggily.

'Well…hello, Sleepy Head! I've been looking all over for you!' He recognised her voice and a sharp jolt rocked his body. He had forgotten all about her existence because of the events of the previous day. 'Are you trying to hide from me or something? She teased. He could imagine her slowly smiling.

'Look, I'm sorry,' he said, 'Something's happened. I'll explain later. I arrived home this morning and had to have a sleep.' It suddenly struck him that she was blatantly calling his mobile. 'Anyway, how did you get my number?'

'Easy! I had that information before I had you!' She laughed and the smile which started off in his eyes spread to his lips.

'You're irrepressible!' he said.

'And that's why you like me,' Andrea replied, 'I'll see you later.' And without waiting for a reply, she ended the call. He thought about her for a moment waiting to feel self-reproach but there was none. It was no more than the Blonde deserved.

The call had given him a warm feeling so he bathed and dressed. He even managed to sing to himself on his way to the office and there she was, waiting in the car park. She was sitting on a wall, swinging her legs like a teenager, her hair blowing in the breeze, accompanied in rhythm by a white silk scarf which was tied round her neck. He smiled at the vision as she came to meet him.

'Since you stood me up at lunchtime,' she giggled, 'I'm going to cook you a meal tonight! How's that for starters?'

'Sounds good to me,' he said, taking her arm, soft and warm, as he guided her through the stationary vehicles, regardless of who might see them together.

'Something Japanese, I think!' she made the statement, her face set in a firm line which flowed down to her ample breasts, clothed in a fine wool material which clung to their outline.

'Japanese what?' he teased.

'Japanese food!' She looked straight into his eyes and he was awestruck. He felt he had known her all his life. He felt so at ease in her company. In the short time he had been aware of her, she had never ceased to amaze him. She seemed to have powers which could sense how he felt and adjust immediately.

Later, at her flat, he felt almost at home. Michael Bublé sang out from her music centre, soothing his whole body. She never asked if it was his kind of music, she just assumed and he didn't mind. He lay back on the sofa, his tie undone, his sleeves rolled back and a glass of wine in his hand. He felt good, better than he had done for a long time and he drowned in the warmth of this feeling, not wanting to lose it for a second.

Smells of exotic cooking came from the kitchen. Spices and herbs mingled into an aroma which made his taste buds fizz.

'It won't be long, darling!' she called from the kitchen. He didn't even mind the familiarity of the word 'darling' as it seemed to fit. A moment later, she came into the room dressed in a Kimono robe, her hair clipped up on top of her head like a Geisha girl. He smiled. Her robe was black and embroidered all over with flamboyant birds, trees, mountains, right down to her bare feet.

'Wow! You look amazing!' he whispered. She moved slowly towards him and the silky gown shone as it caught the light. As she got closer he could see her nipples protruding and he knew she was wearing nothing underneath. She sat beside him and he kissed her naked neck then pulled the clasp from her hair and it fell in streams round her shoulders. He sighed with pleasure as his hand progressed down her body and inside the kimono where he cupped her warm breast. He was hungry for her. Then he traced the outline of her bottom with his fingers. He moved lower, his hand sliding between her legs. He wanted her now and she wanted him and they made love on the sofa until they were both sated. Philip lay back speechless. He had never known pleasure like this. He never wanted it to end and tried to ignore the buzzing next to his ear. It was his mobile. Andrea stretched across and looked at the display. It was the Blonde ringing. She smiled. Her plan was working perfectly.

'Do you want to answer this?' she asked offering him the phone. He shook his head slowly then pulled her towards him and kissed her. She smiled cheekily. 'That was your Hors d'oeuvres!'

He laughed and she made her way to the kitchen.

'I don't know how you do it,' he said as he refilled their wine glasses, 'We only spoke about having dinner a few hours ago!'

'And I only bought everything and prepared it yesterday!' she replied.

'Yesterday? But how…?'

'How did I know? I knew you would come because I knew you'd be unable to resist! Simple!' She leaned over and stroked his cheek. She was right, Philip thought, I can't resist her. 'I'll just check the prawns!' and she jumped up making for the door then turned. 'By the way, the chicken takes at least eight hours to marinate!' then she disappeared. He smiled and he was beginning to enjoy smiling. In the past, he felt that he had little to smile about but now the action was slowly being reborn in him.

The meal was superb. Soft music, warm room, lovely atmosphere and the most beautiful, exciting woman opposite him. He felt very lucky as he started to eat the deep-fried honeyed prawns, little chunks of golden batter, smothered in sesame seeds, which crunched and melted in his mouth.

'Actually, I've cheated a little. This recipe is Chinese!' she said, making him warm to her even more. The serving dishes were pure Japanese porcelain, delicate forms, the light shining through their transparency. The chicken melted in his mouth, light and succulent strips of meat soaked in a sweet, gingery sauce. Then they finished with a traditional English dessert which she had drowned in brandy. It dissolved like melted snow. When they had finished, he took her hand and asked, 'Where do you get the time to learn all this,' gesturing towards the remains of the meal, 'as well as being beautiful every time we meet and not just first thing in the morning?'

She looked at him seriously.

'I make time,' she said simply, 'I intend to be the perfect wife someday...' And she looked beyond him to a vision which she held, a fanatical brilliance lighting her eyes before she returned his gaze, 'as well as the perfect mistress!'

She never ceased to amaze him. On first impressions he had thought her spoilt and superficial, too beautiful to be real, but as time passed, he found there was much more to her. He was alarmed to some extent, unable to analyse exactly what her secret ingredient might be. She seemed perfect, if such a person existed. It seemed that within her lay a force which could achieve anything she wanted and it would not be luck or fate or chance which obtained it for her but planning her whole being to perfection. Philip would never realise how close he was to the truth.

She looked at him with pleasure in her eyes for his compliments and grasped her chance.

'Now tell me what happened last night!'

How could he refuse, feeling intoxicated with the evening and her presence? He recounted details of the call telling him about Leonie and what happened when the Blonde returned. It was difficult for him to tell Andrea about the Blonde's unfaithfulness. It hurt. He felt he was betraying a confidence but once he started talking, he found it impossible to stop, the words pouring from him, rendering some relief. She listened in silence, watching his emotions pass from anger to compassion and all the time she was planning in her head. So far, things had worked out well for her. She just needed the Blonde to want Philip again.

Her face showed no emotion and when he had finished she said, 'And you still love her?' His eyes darted upwards, surveying her quizzically while she continued. 'She's taken you for a ride and you sit there, willing to forgive her and try again.'

He said nothing. He supposed she spoke the truth and maybe he needed an outsider to make him realise how much he had been deceived. He still loved the Blonde, idolised her and even though the past years had been difficult, he imagined it was a phase which they would grow out of together making them stronger. They would look back on this time remembering it as being necessary for them to grow closer. But that was before he was betrayed.

'Leave her,' she whispered quietly at first and then more passionately as she held onto the table making the wine glasses clink together and the dishes vibrate. 'Leave her before it's too late! Now's your chance. Take it!'

Her eyes blazed and looked like a demon's. For an instant he felt afraid of her power over him but just as suddenly, she became a kitten again, pretending to be submissive and he thought he must have been mistaken. She stroked his hair, ran her fingers over his body, arousing desire for her and his previous fears were lost in their abandoned love-making.

Philip stayed at her flat that night and she used the time to her advantage. She ensnared him both physically and mentally so that he was powerless to think and act for himself.

Black Lomax sat in his apartment and read through the script again. The more he read, the more he became convinced that it was a winner. He could visualise himself in the main part, the star of the film this time, no longer in a supporting role. His career was finally beginning to pay dividends and filming was scheduled to start in the States in two months. He played with the corner of a page, reading the lines over and over. It had all been worth the struggle to get to this point in his life. 'The Iowa farm boy had done good!' he thought. He could look back and feel satisfaction from tasks well done, and be able to look forward from his newly elevated position. He had achieved a lot in a short space of time.

Into his thoughts of increasing fame crept the image of the girl he had bumped into unexpectedly earlier in the week. He was puzzled when she stopped him at the Studios and thought at first she might want his autograph but she told him that they had met seven years ago. She had been a fresh faced teenager of sixteen then but the flush of womanhood was already coursing through the curves of her body like a slowly ripening fruit. She reminded him that she had been holidaying with her parents at the palatial Palm Hotel on the West Coast where Black had a job in between acting school. It had not been long before his good looks captured the bored school girl's attention. He smiled now, reliving those hazy memories of years before remembering that her father strongly disapproved of her having any association with an employee of the hotel. But this did not stop them meeting furtively on the beach and eventually, inevitably, having sex on the sand.

He had been little more than a child himself with little knowledge of life but he was her first, he could tell. He remembered the thrill of her warm, virgin body against his as she eagerly gave herself to him. It became a habit during her stay that she would sneak out of her room after dark when Black finished his shift and they would meet on the beach. He had thought of it as a holiday romance and when her summer came to an end, he was prepared to move on to his next youthful conquest.

They were energetic days when the world was new and open to discovery. She had obviously thought differently and he vaguely remembered her tears when they said goodbye. He remembered too their promises to write and to keep in touch. He had written once but somehow there seemed no point in continuing the charade of replying to her letters which were filled with protestations of love and undying affection which he found impossible to return by letter or any other means. He had moved on and imagined that memories of that summer would probably be just as embarrassing for her as they were for him. He laughed aloud.

Eventually, her letters stopped arriving and the months passed and Black had been relieved. He imagined that she, like himself, had moved on to other romances and their brief affair had been buried in the passing of time.

She was much more sophisticated now, no longer the child, but a beautiful woman. No longer a clinging vine eager to please him at any cost to gain his affection. He imagined she was now an independent woman who knew exactly how to achieve her objectives.

He thought it peculiar but he had completely forgotten her name after all those years and felt slightly embarrassed that she used his without hesitation when they met. Of course, she could have seen one of his films or perhaps on a chat show on television. It certainly was a small world and strange that they should meet at the television studios. He wondered what the odds against it were. What was her name? He found his mobile and searched his contacts. There it was. Andy. That was it. He said the name over and over trying to remember using it but he couldn't. He remembered it as a pet name and thought she would have disposed of it as readily as she had disposed of childhood. They planned to meet again soon and the prospect excited Black.

The opposite sex had played a large part in Black's life since the first burst of manhood had flowed through his body, hardening the smooth lines of his face, broadening the slim frame. At sixteen, he had stood six feet tall and could pass for a young man in his early twenties. As a result, early in his life he had been propositioned by a variety of older women unaware of his tender age although there were some who feigned ignorance. He had been flattered but never tempted by their efforts to seduce him. He was a handsome youth with a generous, firm mouth, his smile being an immediate source of attraction. His nose was straight and in proportion but a slight bump obtained when playing baseball, added character to his features. His face was framed by a mop of deepest black, thick hair which followed the curves of his head in thick waves.

There had always been women in his life waiting for him to notice their existence and his youth had been punctuated with affairs which had varied in their intensity from compatible warmth to unconcerned passion. In all, he had never shown himself as thoughtless or hurtful but sensitive and honest, endearing himself even more to those who realised that any sort of permanent liaison with him was not their destiny. Black had many female friends, victims of this fate but their regard for him was so high that they had remained friendly over the years in the knowledge that it was better to have a small part of him than none at all. It gave them a feeling of comfort and also a particle of hope. As time passes, feelings and emotions change so one day they might find they were the object of renewed interest in his life.

He thought about all of them, their faces over the years blending into a collage, the features merging into each other and the final version being the Blonde. His stomach churned over as he allowed himself the thrill of visualising her. He was like a child stealing a last look at his story book before lights out. He smiled to himself. She was the epitome of everything and everyone who had been the fabric of his life to date. For the first time, he no longer held the relationship at a safe distance but wanted to crush it to his body until it became as much a part of him as life itself. He was in love although the word unsettled him because of its indefinable qualities but he knew that he needed her and had never needed anyone so desperately in his whole life.

His phone rang breaking into the solitude of his thoughts. After a second's hesitation to bring him back to reality, he answered.

'Black?' her voice sounded soft but there was an urgency to it! 'Oh, Black, thank God I've got you at last. The most awful thing has happened…'

'Hey! Slow down, Babe!' He interrupted. 'Where are you?'

'I'm at my sister's house…' she said, her voice trembling as he again interrupted impatiently.

'I've been trying to get a hold of you, Honey! I'm so glad to hear you. What's happened?'

She recounted the events leading to her presence at Leonie's, about Philip waiting for her at the house when she left Black after their last weekend together and when she had finished talking, she began to sob quietly.

'The bastard! He hit you? I'll kill him!' Black yelled. He felt helpless, wanting to take her in his arms and comfort her. 'Look, Honey, don't cry. Do you want me to come down? I could be there in an hour or so.'

It was tempting. She needed comfort and reassurance in her loneliness but felt that further complications would only add to her distress.

'No, please don't, Black. Jeff's in pieces! I have to work things out for myself. I tried to contact Philip but he doesn't seem to be at the house. I've tried early morning and late at night but can't get a hold of him. I can't think where he can be. It's not like him.'

'You wanna contact him after he's done that to you? He's a mean bastard!'

'I know but…' She started to make excuses for Philip, blaming everything on herself but he stopped her.

'Look, now that he's discovered there's someone else, why not tell him the whole story. Tell him you're leaving for the States with me!'

There followed a long silence during which she could hear his gentle breathing as though he were standing next to her.

'Black, I haven't decided yet. I don't know if I can come with you after what's happened.'

He was deeply hurt. For the first time in his life he would have to beg and plead to realise his aim. This time he was on the receiving end of a relationship and the Blonde held all the power.

'Honey,' his voice was soft and persuasive, 'I'm serious about this. I want you to come with me and when things get sorted out and we're settled, I want us to get married!'

She sighed visualising their married state and seeing it disintegrating over time, making her alone again, Black having moved on with all his energies intact. The little confidence she was now left with did not stretch to imagine Black being content to spend the rest of his life with her.

'Give me just a little bit longer, Black. I'll call you when I get back to London.'

It was Black's turn to sigh.

'OK. Kitten,' he said resignedly, 'but make it soon. I love you.'

The words cut into her. He had rarely used them before and this made her feel committed to him. She felt herself being pulled in two directions, powerless to decide where her future lay.

# Ten

The days passed slowly, some rainy, some sunny but all generally dull for the Blonde. She was frustrated. She began to feel like a prisoner of her own guilt. Living amongst the remnants of a broken marriage each day, she saw her time spent at Leonie's as a penance for past transgressions and no matter how hard she tried to feel grateful for everything, the burden lay heavily upon her. She longed to be back to normality, to put all this behind her and live her life freely. She began to think that her existence was not so bad in reality. Philip could be boring at times but maybe this was made worse by the fact that she had nothing to interest her. A year ago, she had a freelance design career which she could pick up or drop whenever she wanted. She didn't need to work. Philip made enough money for both of them and he liked the thought of her being at home. It was an old fashioned idea of his because he wanted a family. At first, she didn't mind being there. It was a change to the hustle of working life with all its competitiveness and bitching but lately, she had plenty of time to consider her life and crave change. When that opportunity had arisen in the form of Black, she had seized it eagerly.

Now her days were composed of watching Jeff work on his scheme for the house even though Leonie had refused to see him at the hospital. The Blonde had to act as 'go between' and tactfully tried to dissuade him from his plans.

'Jeff, do you really think that all you are doing is going to make a difference to how Leonie feels now?'

He stopped sweeping shavings of wall paper which the decorator's hoover had missed and looked at her with a quizzical expression on his face.

'You don't know what Leonie and I had going!' He sounded almost angry that she could question him. 'We've been together years. Leonie wouldn't throw all that away.'

She thought he must be deluded. Was it arrogance which motivated him? She needed to make him understand how Leonie was feeling.

'But Leonie said...!' He stopped her by putting his hand up to show he didn't want to hear any more.

'She's still recovering!' he said snappily, 'Give her time to come to her senses!'

The Blonde was angry on her sister's behalf but maybe Jeff was right. Maybe she didn't know how much they meant to each other. She was determined to find out from Leonie when she visited the hospital that evening.

Leonie sat, fully clothed, on a chair next to her hospital bed. The nurses were encouraging her to take little walks round the wards to build her strength and confidence. The dark circles had gone from her eyes and her pallor was normal.

'You'll be going home soon,' the Blonde smiled encouragingly, 'And Jeff will be there.'

'He better not be!' Leonie said quickly.

The Blonde thought she had better raise the subject of their relationship.

'I thought you missed him so much?' she questioned tentatively.

'I did in the beginning. I was in shock! In here, I've had time to think and I can't forgive what he did.' She sounded strong and resolute. 'I would always be thinking about it and never be able to let go. I don't want to live like that, always bitter, living with the constant reminder of it! He'll have to move out when I come back.'

The Blonde told her how he had employed decorators to paint the kitchen and had plans for other improvements which she had always wanted. Leonie was angry.

'If he thinks a touch of paint and a few new units are going to make a difference, he's sadly mistaken! I might have welcomed that before all this happened but not now. What's done is done and there's no going back!' Her voice got louder. 'I don't even want to see him! You can tell him I want him out before I get home.' She leaned over towards the Blonde and said quietly, 'Can you tell him, please? I thought he would get the message after I said I didn't want to see him but obviously not.'

The Blonde nodded. She would tell him. She owed Leonie that at least but she still felt sick at the prospect. She really did not want to be involved but it was too late to back out.

When she entered the house, Jeff was standing there, expectantly.

'Well? How was she?' he asked impatiently.

'She's well... getting back on her feet. She's walking around and hopes to get out soon!' the Blonde said hesitantly as she took off her coat and hung it in the hall.

'Brilliant! I can't wait to have her back home!' he said then noticed her expression. 'What's wrong?'

She was quiet for a moment, not knowing how to broach the subject then she decided it was best just to blurt it out.

'Leonie doesn't want you to be here, Jeff! She wants you to be gone before she gets back.'

He looked stunned and his facial expression changed from anticipation to desolation. He struggled to find a chair and sat down heavily. His face crumpled and his body deflated like a burst balloon. He looked a poor imitation of the man she had left that morning. He looked up at her with watery, red eyes.

'But what about the children? How is she going to manage?

'Don't worry about the children,' she said softly, 'Leonie has arranged all that.'

He looked into the far distance at nothing at all.

'I'm finished...' he cried and stood up noisily from the table. She tried to reassure him with empty phrases which did not help to placate him. 'If she doesn't want me here, then I won't be here!' he cried, grabbing his jacket and thundering upstairs. She could hear the screech of cupboard doors opening and drawers closing as he collected his belongings and flung them in a case. He could hardly look in her direction before he left.

'Bye. I hope things work out for you,' he said and then was gone.

The Blonde felt sorry for him. Life was a game; one great, big game and they were all in it together, playing out the odds, sometimes winning, sometimes losing but always striving to reach their goal.

Leonie would be coming home soon and she would leave. She had offered to stay longer but Leonie was adamant that she would manage as she had employed a live-in nanny who would help with the children and be company for her. At last she was free to return home.

The Blonde unlocked the door to the darkened house, the scent of emptiness hitting her immediately. A dark, damp odour hung in the hallway as though the place hadn't been heated for a while. As she switched on the light, she noticed that a thin film of dust covered everything. It had only been a short time, but everywhere she looked seemed so unfamiliar. Leaving her case in the hall, she cautiously opened the door to the lounge. There was no sign of Philip having been there recently. No newspaper lying carelessly on a chair. No empty glass left or even a discarded tie. Jeff and Leonie's relationship breakdown had shocked her. She thought she might try to make amends with Philip but it was probably too late. Her own selfishness had destroyed everything he had ever felt for her.

As she was about to gather her belongings, she heard a key turning in the lock. It was Philip. He looked at her in surprise and she felt she was trespassing. Her first instinct was to smile, to run to him and tell him it had all been a big mistake but she was frozen to the spot. He seemed surprised.

'I wasn't expecting to see you here,' he said, not looking in her direction.

'I tried to phone you…' she stammered, 'but you never answered your mobile. Where were you?'

He laid an overnight bag on the floor and stood looking at her, a long empty stare. His face was serious.

'I've just come to collect a few shirts and things. I'm not staying!'

She tried to control the cold fear which gripped her insides like an icy hand.

'Oh, Phillip, please...' she said softly noticing his pained expression, 'Please stay. We can talk!'

He hesitated as if he were about to say something then turned away from her.

'Don't give me any more of your shit! I've had enough!' he said speaking to the floor as he struggled to unzip his bulging overnight bag. She was silenced. He was slipping away from her. He turned to look for a reaction but there was none. 'Look, I might as well be straight with you,' he continued, 'God knows why I should...but there's someone else. I've been staying at her place! And she's warm and wonderful,' and he spat out, 'Everything you're not!'

It was as though he had hit her again, the power of his words devastating her. He strode past her and up the stairs.

'When? How?' she muttered after him but he did not look back. She could hear him open the wardrobe, hear coat hangers being scraped along the rail as he searched for some particular piece of clothing. Then he started to open drawers and she could visualise him taking out the freshly laundered shirt that she had given him for Christmas. She could see him wearing it while the hands of another woman, a headless apparition, caressed his body clothed in her present. She felt giddy, the walls closing in around her and a nauseating darkness clouded her mind. Eerie shapes formed in front of her eyes accompanying the throbbing in her head. She tried to shut them out but they persisted, driving an overwhelming jealousy through her.

Feeling for the door of the lounge, she groped her way to the drinks cabinet. A sip of whisky and the feeling started to come back to her wretched frame. Sitting on the sofa, she saw their life together pass before her and the full consequences of what she had done hit her harder than usual. They were all lying to each other. Lies. Big, buttery lies.

His voice dragged her back to the present.

'I'm off now,' he said casually as though he were going out for a bit,' If there's anything you need, ring my secretary.'

She nodded and could hear the door close behind him.

Once again she found herself alone in the silence. She could not cry although she desperately wanted to unburden herself. She sat impassively, thinking about her husband with another woman. Where could he have met her? He never went out. It was so out of character for Philip. Suddenly she had an idea. Running through to his study, she threw herself into a feverish search of his papers. Almost gleefully her fingers tore at the pages of his desk diary, screwing up the corners as she frantically searched for a particle of evidence but there was nothing except business appointments. She studied his letters feeling like a common criminal but these all contained only what she imagined they would, business.

Her mind became a thrashing sea and she was a fish swimming frantically back and forth. She hurried to the bedroom and looked at his clothes to see if she could tell which he had taken but she found that most of them were unfamiliar to her. Had she really watched him leave for work in these shirts and never noticed them? Her eyes fell on the lid of the clothes basket which was half open as he had left some clothes for washing. The thought amused her. Only a man could leave so many loose ends. Perhaps this was only a temporary parting. After all, why shouldn't he have his revenge if that was his motive? She had no grounds for complaint.

Lifting the basket lid, she picked up the shirt which had been left on top and pressed the soft material to her face. It smelt vaguely of his aftershave mingled with a perfume she did not recognise. Her eyes stung, her throat tightened and tears trickled down her cheeks onto the soft material which absorbed them like blotting paper. She stayed this way for some time thinking about him and was about to drop the shirt back into the basket when she felt something crinkle in the pocket. Hurriedly, she dug her fingers into the opening and extracted a small, crumpled piece of paper. Trembling hands unravelled it. There in small, round handwriting were the words 'Andrea Winbech, 46 Cambridge Mansions,' and a mobile number. She thought her heart would stop beating. So she was real after all, not just existing in Philip's imagination. Envy consumed her. Refolding the paper carefully, she thought again and crushed it in her hand about to throw it in the waste bin but something stopped her. She hesitated as the idea formed in her mind. Unravelling the tatty ball, she carefully read the information again. Finding her mobile, she angrily punched in the number. Her head felt heavy and she steadied her body as she waited for a reply. It rang continuously for some time and she was about to end the call when a young woman answered.

'Andrea here.'

Her voice was bathed in an innocent seductiveness. There followed a loud silence.

'Hello!' she repeated, sounding irritated but the Blonde did not answer. She ended the call and stared into space. The headless apparition she had imagined now had a name and a voice and Philip.

Without warning, she heard the front door opening. Immediately she thought that Phillip had changed his mind and returned. She eagerly ran downstairs, ready to hug him but was crushed when she saw Peggy Watts standing in the hallway.

'Oh, My Lord! Whatever's happened to you?' Peggy saw the devastation and disappointment in the Blonde's face and put an arm round her. 'Come on, love, into the kitchen and I'll make you a nice cuppa and you can tell me all about it!'

She propelled the Blonde into the room and onto a chair while she made tea.

Peggy had been cleaning for the Blonde and Phillip for the last three years. She lived across the road so it had been convenient when the Blonde was working to have her prepare an evening meal, do some washing and keep the place tidy. She was in her fifties, a 'salt of the earth' type with a ruddy complexion and striking blue eyes. Peggy and she had become friends and she still helped out regularly when needed.

'Now tell me what it's all about,' Peggy said, easing her plump, motherly frame into a chair at the kitchen table.

The Blonde always felt at ease in her company and knew that she could tell her anything with no fear of it being repeated outside the house. She was dependable so they left a key with her.

'Phillip's left me!' she wailed.

''E's done what?' Peggy exclaimed, an expression of surprise on her face. The Blonde sipped the hot tea and tried to stop trembling. 'Left you? Surely not! I can't believe it!

You always seemed very 'appy to me. Perfect little couple, I thought!' The Blonde said nothing. 'You think 'e'll come back then?'

'No, I think it's final. He told me he's found someone else.'

'Well, don't upset yourself so. No man's worth that amount of tears!'

The Blonde managed a half smile and Peggy wondered if she should say something or not then she decided she would.

'It's funny you should say that 'cos the other night I was putting out my bins when Phillip's car drew up. Mind you, only next to the pavement. He didn't come all the way into the drive so I could see his car clearly. He went into the house and there was a woman sitting in the passenger's seat. She never got out, you know. I had to look twice and thought to myself 'that ain't his wife!' then I thought it might be a relation 'cos she looked a lot younger than him. Long red hair and a haughty look.' The Blonde looked interested. 'I didn't like the look of her. Straightaways, I said to myself, she's a bad un but thought it was none of my business so just went back indoors. When I looked later, the car had gone and the house was in darkness.' So he had brought her here to their territory. Anger replaced regret as Peggy continued. 'And another thing…last week I came in to do my bit, you know, dust and polish, keep the place tidy while you were down at your sister's but he appeared and told me not to bother! Just like that! Well, I can tell you I was taken aback! After all the years I been with you! He didn't do it friendly like or anything, just said 'you're not needed.' Well, you know my temper and I got mad and said, 'Wot you mean, not needed? You ain't talking to your secretary now, you know!' He stared

113

daggers at me and said that you might not be back and there was no point and I could give him my key. Well, I was bloody furious by then and said, 'You ain't getting my key! She gave me the key and she's the one who'll get it back!' Once Peggy started talking it was difficult for her to stop but the Blonde listened intently. 'I tell you, I saw another side to Phillip that day!'

Peggy refilled their cups while the Blonde related the events of the last few weeks.

'So you see,' she uttered with a voice which broke with emotion, 'It's not entirely Phillip's fault. He found out when Leonie...' She couldn't bear to say the words.

Peggy looked concerned and said, 'Well, I don't blame you finding this other fellow. As I said, I saw another side of Phillip and one that I didn't like at all. I always thought he was easy going but you can never tell until you live with them day in and day out. I should know! I've been married twice and never again!'

'I'm sorry he treated you like that, Peggy. He had no right. He shouldn't have taken his anger and bitterness out on you. He didn't know what my plans were,' the Blonde said quietly.

'If I were you, I'd take the bull by the horns and get out! That's all I'm going to say but you know I'm here for you if you need me.' She hesitated for a moment. 'Now I think you should get up to bed and 'av a nice long sleep! I'll come back later and rustle up something nice for your tea. How does that sound?'

The Blonde reached over to give her a hug.

'That sounds wonderful, Peggy! What would I do without you?'

# Eleven

Black Lomax looked at his watch as he sat at the hotel bar. He was becoming irritable. The table was reserved for eight and it was past that time already. He ordered another Scotch. If there was one thing he was a stickler for it was punctuality. He hated to be kept waiting and, as a result, saw to it that he never kept anyone waiting for him. He stood up and stretched his legs in the foyer, proceeding to walk back and forth, counting the squares on the large red carpet which lined the area. People were beginning to stare at him and he felt like a teenager who had been stood up on his first date.

Five past, ten past, quarter past eight. His eyes darted from the large wall clock to the entrance doors. Just as he had decided to ring her number, she appeared. She looked spectacular. All eyes turned her way. Oblivious to them, she walked towards him, a hint of arrogance in her step. He left his drink and moved to meet her. Her long auburn hair had been swept back and shone like wet gold. A cream coat highlighted the dark beauty of her eyes set in olive skin.

'I'm sorry I'm late,' she whispered breathlessly, adding to the overwhelming effect her appearance was having on him. 'The traffic was terrible and my taxi driver got lost in the one-way system.'

Her eyes were stunning, glowing like embers and her speech was punctuated by inviting smiles which would have softened the stoniest resolve. He was captivated by her beauty. Surely this could not be the same girl he had met by chance last week, far less the teenager of seven years before. Amazed that he had failed to notice so much about her, he did not speak but allowed her to continue so that he could listen to her richly sensuous voice.

He guided her towards the restaurant, a feeling of warmth and intimacy rising in his body as he touched her. He slipped the coat from her shoulders, watching the strands of auburn hair reset themselves as she flung the mane backwards and ran her fingers through its long abundance. He noticed her slender neck and the flawless skin of her back as it disappeared under the low cut of her dress.

Black felt light headed. Having to wait he had consumed a few more drinks than he intended. A waiter ushered them to their table.

'This way, Mr Lomax.'

Chandeliers dotted the ceiling like stars in a night sky while an orchestra played soft music somewhere in the distance, sending a feeling of calm throughout the air, creating just the right atmosphere.

She walked ahead following the waiter, her body undulating with every step she took. The flimsy material of her black dress clung tightly to her body like another skin. It stretched over her thighs and stopped just above the knee to reveal long legs of perfect proportion. A single pearl clasp was attached to the neck of her dress where the material had been slashed across at the front, enveloping her breasts. The effect was simple and dramatic. Eyes turned to watch the little group weaving its way through the tables and, aware of the effect she was creating, she played to her audience with added haughtiness and total indifference as though unaware of their existence. Black felt good. He admired a woman with style and she certainly had it as far as he was concerned. He enjoyed being in the company of a beautiful woman and watch men's envious eyes follow him.

When they were seated, waiters busied around them with menus and wine lists while shaking out freshly laundered, stiff white napkins. Black grew impatient. He wanted her to himself. He barely looked at the delicacies on offer, ordering the first dish available and a large bottle of the best wine. In contrast, she took her time, changing her mind occasionally, speaking her thoughts aloud and deliberating over the choice of each course because she knew that he was watching her. When she had chosen, the waiters left them alone and Black leaned over the table towards her.

'You really should have let me pick you up this evening instead of relying on a taxi.' He smiled warmly. She thought for a moment before speaking.

'It was no trouble except it made me late!' she smiled, 'Anyway, there's nothing more off-putting than knowing that your date is waiting in the next room agitatedly looking at his watch while you dress!' She smiled and looked away from him, studying the other diners, eager to know if her entrance was still having an effect. Those sitting in close proximity were surreptitiously looking in her direction under the watchful eyes of their female companions who were also finding it difficult not to sneak an envious glance at the beautiful redhead.

Over the meal they talked about the coincidence of meeting again after all those years.

'What you doing with yourself these days?' he asked as the waiter refilled their wine glasses.

'I wasn't doing much until a few months ago when my father found me a job at the studios, the studios where you are making your television programme.' She waited for a reaction. His face showed surprise. He thought it was peculiar that they had both ended up in the same place after all these years but he didn't mention it.

'I remember your father, Winston Elliot Winbech III. How could I forget him! And he recalled his dealings with the bluff, 'no nonsense' tycoon who threatened him.

'Leave my daughter alone!' he had shouted. 'How much will it take?' he had asked, removing his wallet from inside his jacket. 'A guy like you must need money or you wouldn't be waiting at tables!' He had started to count out the dollar bills but Black refused to be bought. He had been angry and insulted at the time but now his face was animated as he recalled that summer seven years ago. Her father hadn't frightened Black and they continued their clandestine meeting on the beach after dark. He felt bad about it now so made excuses for not writing, not keeping in touch and, for an instant, he thought he saw her calm resolve slip and noticed two tiny patches of pink appear on her olive cheeks and a dullness entering her eyes. Maybe he was imagining it.

They continued to talk, updating each other about how they had spent the last years, peppering their conversation with little anecdotes which the other might find amusing. But neither was really interested in this small talk, their minds wandering along a different track from the current conversation.

The evening passed pleasantly while the orchestra continued to play soft, romantic music in the background. Black felt mellow. As a rule he did not drink very much alcohol but as the meal progressed, he had been oblivious to the amount of wine he had consumed on top of Scotch, and now felt very light headed, longing to hold her in his arms. When he saw figures cradled together in the dim light, swaying to the music, he suggested they dance. He held her closely, gently, like something precious, afraid that she might shatter in is grasp. Her body moved with his and her unusual perfume, which seemed to touch all of her, floated up to him, firing his spirit. He caressed her soft hair with his lips and a breathless feeling of anticipation absorbed him as her small, delicate hands draped themselves round his neck.

When the music stopped, they sat down. Her face was flushed like a slowly ripening peach. She looked radiant. As she breathed, the black dress, stretched across her breasts, moved like waves lapping against the shore. He desired her now as he had never done before. He smiled inwardly remembering their tentative love-making of years before. This time it would be different, a consummation of all those nights of gathered experience since then.

Outside in the fresh night air, as street and car lights lit the gloom, he called for his chauffeur and asked her, 'Your place or mine for a night cap?'

'Yours;' she replied quickly, 'My father's visiting me for a few days and I wouldn't like to disturb him. He goes to bed early these days!' She smiled wryly as she thought about Phillip back at Cambridge Mansions, waiting for her.

Black gave his driver instructions and they sped through the city. It was late now and the streets were fairly empty. She lay in his arms watching the lights flash by and felt at peace. He was even more desirable than she remembered, if that was possible, and he was to be hers for tonight and for as long as she wanted him.

He snuggled up to her, tentatively touching her breasts under the cream coat then more confidently whispering, 'Andy…' urgently in her ear.

'I don't use that name now,' she said quietly, running her fingers round the back of his neck, firing him with desire, 'I've outgrown it. It's Andrea…' and he silenced her with a kiss.

Once inside his apartment, Black poured her a drink and one for himself but it never touched his lips, his desire for her being so immediate. He kissed her feverishly, his hands weaving patterns over her body which flowed into her brain. He pushed her gently onto his bed and she helped him remove her clothes so that he could feel her warm, inviting flesh beneath his hands. Soon he was inside her and their coming together was a rapidly lustful sensation which he had never before experienced in its intensity. Black lay back satisfied.

Later, he thought about the Blonde and an ache consumed him but he reasoned that he had no hold over her, a married woman, except what she felt for him and that was still to be proven. He knew he had drunk too much and still felt woozy. His reasoning was askew. It seemed so long since he had seen the Blonde. Why shouldn't he spend the days in between with congenial female company if she wasn't there? He needed reassurance and comfort. What man didn't?

Sometime in the early morning, with a heavy head, he pulled his naked body from the bed, stood up and stretched. He felt fragile and, as he looked at her sleeping, the whole evening came thundering back to him in one great big ball of guilt. He had tried to justify his actions but he still felt bad.

'Morning, darling!' a tiny voice emerged from under the covers.

It was unexpected and Black was snatched back to reality. He flinched at her use of the word 'darling'. It was too intimate. He had to say something but didn't know what in the cool light of day. He wanted her gone.

'Hey, Babe, I thought you were still asleep!' he managed to mutter groggily. She turned in the bed to face him and raised herself on one elbow. He could see the smooth line of her breasts, their full firmness falling to the pillow and he remembered how soft and warm they were.

'Why don't you come back to bed?' she said enticingly, 'It's still early?'

He looked towards the window and could see that the sun had hardly risen in the sky. The sound of traffic hadn't built up and the day wasn't yet awake. He had to think fast.

'Sorry, Honey, much as I'd love to, I've got a meeting today.' It was the best he could do.

'What? On a Saturday?' She sounded annoyed.

'Yeah. It's a sorta lunch/brunch meeting. I gotta have a shower, Babe. You help yourself to coffee and whatever you want,' Black said dismissively as he headed for the shower room. Andrea lay simmering. This wasn't meant to happen. It was meant to turn out differently and she pounded the duvet with her fist, anger bursting from every pore.

# Twelve

The outside was decorated with elaborate yellow and orange canopies which masked the windows from the summer sun and served the dual purpose of concealing the patrons. The interior was restful. Distressed wooden tables stretched round the walls which had large windows cut from them at regular intervals. At the back, an open plan staircase led to another level. Soft cushions covered the high backed benches and metallic lamps hung low over each table creating a dim glow of intimacy. To add to the feeling of seclusion, large, potted plants shrouded each table from the gaze of pedestrians. Soft music streamed through speakers interspersed by the click-clack of customer's heels on the tiled floor against the low hum of conversation. It was exclusive and secluded. That's why they had chosen it as there was little chance of being discovered. Occasionally, when she had been there with Black they had heard a quiet whispering of his name. 'Black Lomax, isn't it?' or 'Isn't that what's his name… Black Lomax,' but no one ever bothered them or interrupted their privacy.

Each article fitted into the overall illusion. Grey pottery cups and saucers sat invitingly on the polished counter while golden crusty granules of sugar over flowed hospitably from buff clay bowls. Trays of delicacies were stacked high. Crusty croissants and granary rolls piled temptingly next to thick slabs of wholemeal apple and raisin flan topped with swirls of fresh cream and cherries the size of marbles. The atmosphere was rich with wholesomeness.

The Blonde looked through the chinks in the leaves of a Cheese Plant to the concrete world outside. A solitary tree had been saved amongst the mass of square, lifeless buildings in the City. Gripped by the breeze, its leaves wavered now, floating silently across its moving surface. It was cold outside, the last of the summer having been devoured by a new season. Some leaves were still green but already autumn had touched their tips painting them in her familiar rust colours. The tree seemed to be preparing itself for this transformation, eager to shed its dying burden and rejuvenate in the coming year. Pieces of discarded rubbish were being whipped along by the wind while pigeons swooped towards the window in their search for food. Shoppers sauntered slowly along in groups and the lights from offices in the covered walk, glowed in the daylight. The energies displayed in the summer had died now. Hibernation was settling in.

The Blonde turned from the outside scene and checked her phone. No text. No missed calls. Where was he? She had waited half an hour after their arranged time. Normally, he was very punctual and she suddenly felt uneasy. People were beginning to notice her sitting alone drinking coffee so she decided to leave. Quickly gathering her things together, she made for the exit. Just then a familiar face entered but it wasn't Black. They stood for a moment looking at each other. She hardly recognised Eduardo Costello. He was wearing a leather jacket with a fur trimmed collar which was turned up, jeans and a ski hat which covered his hair. His eyes were obscured by dark glasses.

'Hi there!' he said flamboyantly, blocking her exit. 'You're Phil Mason's wife, aren't you?'

He was tall, handsome and very charming.

'Yes,' she replied quietly not thinking that he would ever remember her from the few occasions when they had been introduced. He turned to his companion.

'Allow me to introduce Brett Schaeffer. Brett deals with everything for me!' Brett was dark and slim with an easy smile which made her feel at ease. They shook hands. 'Hey! You're not leaving, are you? Gee, you gotta come and have some refreshment with us. We've been sightseeing—been round St Paul's. It's fascinating but I need a drink now!'

Without waiting for an answer, Eduardo guided her to a table. She supposed she was not doing anything else that afternoon so why not? She couldn't wait around for Black forever.

They drank coffee and ate and laughed until dusk obscured the buildings opposite and the interior lights became brighter. They made easy conversation and the Blonde found she was relaxing and enjoying herself more than she had done in the previous month. It was good to laugh again. There was no pressure from either of them and Black, Philip and Leonie were forgotten for a couple of hours.

'Hey, guess who I saw at the Ritz yesterday?' Brett said, looking at Eduardo expectantly.

'Well…go on! Who'd you see?'

'Go on! Guess! Geez! You don't know that many people in Britain! Have a guess!'

'I dunno! Brad Pitt?'

'Black Lomax!'

At the mention of his name, the blonde froze.

'No kidding! I've not seen Lomax for weeks. I heard he's making for the States soon.' Eduardo commented.

'Well,' said Brett, 'He looked quite busy to me…had this gorgeous woman with him and they looked pretty cosy!'

The Blonde felt sick. She tried to hide the alarm she felt. Black with a woman! Was that why he had forgotten their appointment? He must be tired waiting for her to make up her mind. Her thoughts were in turmoil. She had tried phoning him but he never picked up. She must see him. Now. There was no time to lose. Eduardo and Brett's conversation seemed far away almost in another dimension as they continued to speculate about the woman with Black. She suddenly rose from her chair, gathered her belongings and excused herself.

'I'm sorry. I've got to go! I've just remembered an appointment!'

Eduardo and Brett looked at each other wondering if they had offended her.

'You OK Honey?' Eduardo called after her, 'We haven't offended you, have we?' She shook her head and tried to smile. 'Make sure you keep in touch! You have my number now so there's no excuse …and meet up soon!' She nodded and almost ran from the building.

Black Lomax woke late. The noise of the traffic on the street below had steadily eaten into his sleep until he became conscious, unable to bear the intrusion any longer. He got out of bed and heard the postman slip something through the letterbox. Sauntering sleepily in his bare feet, he collected the mail. There were the usual typed business letters. He sorted through the pile and threw them aside one by one then his heart lurched as he recognised the writing on a white envelope and realisation hit him. 'Geez,' he thought 'How could I forget! What's happened to me?' He tore open the envelope, a hot sweat developing on his forehead.

'Darling Black,

I waited for you today but you never arrived! I've tried to phone you lots but you never seem to be available. I hope this doesn't mean that you've changed your mind about us because I want to come with you. Ring me, please.'

It was short and to the point. She was going to the States with him. She had decided! He smiled a huge broad smile and congratulated himself. He danced around the room, throwing the typed envelopes over his shoulder. He didn't care if anyone could hear him or imaginary eyes see him. He was happy, contented, care free and he wanted to celebrate.

He read the Blonde's letter over and over again and thought how much he loved her. Only one thing clouded his happiness and he tried to erase it from his mind but it kept emerging more prominently and refused to be eradicated. It was not so much the vision of red strands of hair falling over his face, engulfing him in passion, but more a sickness, like being addicted to a drug and powerless against its potency to give it up.

He found his mobile and frantically punched in her number. He waited impatiently, tapping his foot until she answered.

'Honey!' he called into the phone, his voice overflowing with excitement. 'I've just received your letter, Babe. Hey, you've no idea how great that news is!' and without waiting for her to speak, he continued. 'I'll make all the arrangements today and we can fly out next month. You won't regret this, Baby, I promise you! OK?'

'Yes,' she replied.

'I'll see you later. Oh, look, I'm sorry about yesterday. I've had a lot on my mind lately. I'll explain when I see you. OK if I call about seven? We'll go for a meal.'

'See you about seven.' And she ended the call feeling more contented than she had done for months now that she had made a decision. She saw it as the only road open to her after Philip's indifference. She would have to live with her guilt and take the path which it had built for her but now she had a future and that future was with Black. Even if it meant a few days, a few months or at best, a few years of happiness, it was better than vegetating alone. But there were still doubts. Black had changed since she had been staying at Leonie's and she could not understand why. Everyone around her seemed to be changing and she was being buffeted along with them. When they had first met, he would never have forgotten an appointment with her. He seemed distracted lately. It could be strain of work. She supposed all actors were temperamental, creative and emotional. Why should he be any different? But who was this woman? She would have to find out.

Phillip opened the door of the Cambridge Mansions flat with the key Andrea had given him. Overnight, he had exchanged one life for another. His past was a dim reflection, his present a vacuum and his future undecided.

The red head had been out a lot lately. Her father was in town and she seemed to spend every evening with him. She explained that she felt guilty about her treatment and neglect of him in the past. After all, she reasoned, he was not getting any younger and she wanted to make amends before it was too late. Philip had no desire to complicate his life further by meeting her father. He could understand her feelings and appreciate their need for privacy. At first, he had secretly resented the time she spent apart from him, but, touched by the effort she took to make herself his 'beautiful daughter' with such detail, he forgave her and counted the minutes until she came home to him.

Sometimes, as he sat in lonely isolation, he would try to stop himself from thinking about the Blonde but it was impossible and a yearning crept into his emotions. He tried to suppress it by thinking about something else but she still ate into his thoughts, at times unexpectedly, catching him unaware. He had wanted to contact her, had even stopped himself from phoning just to hear her voice during the long evenings he spent waiting for Andrea but his pride had won and sense prevailed. If she needed him, she would come to him but no matter how much he tried not to admit it, he still missed her.

But all thoughts of the Blonde were dispelled when Andrea arrived home bringing a vitality to the apartment which never failed to cheer him. She would cover him with kisses and demonstrations of how she had missed him and how boring the evening had been without him, how her father would be leaving soon and how they could spend their evenings together again without interruptions. She was childlike in her protestations which poured from her like a waterfall. He just cuddled her and looked patiently on. Andrea knew she was playing a dangerous game with Philip when she left him alone for so long. She watched him closely and sometimes he was back living with the Blonde, arguing with the Blonde, challenging her to love him again. Andrea knew she was running out of options. It was only a question of time before he was back there. She could sense this and the thought that he could be slipping through her grasp, disturbed her. There was only one course of action left.

'Black Lomax!' she said suddenly.

Philip looked at her, his eyes darting back and forth across her face.

'What...?' he asked.

'Black Lomax,' Andrea repeated, her head held high, a look of malice in her eyes. 'That's who she spent the night of Leonie's attempted suicide with! Black Lomax!' She repeated the name enjoying the sound it made and the effect the repetition was having on Philip. His face had turned almost white, almost grey, and she thought he aged considerably as she watched him. He screwed up his eyes and his features contorted as though he had just swallowed a lemon. If he hadn't been there, her desire to laugh would have been fulfilled but she suppressed it and donned the mask of sympathetic compassion. He did not speak, just sat there, staring ahead, his eyes blank.

'Philip,' she said softly, her eyes brimming with tears. 'Philip, I wouldn't have told you but I felt it was your right to know and how could I keep it to myself knowing how torturous it must be for you.'

He turned his head and looked at her blankly as though seeing her for the first time.

'But I know him. We're friends!' Phillip muttered, looking into space. There was a long silence before he asked, 'How long have you known?'

She looked down at his hand which she was holding and stroked it gently. Pretending that it was very difficult for her to explain, she replied hesitantly, 'For…a few months…I suppose, ever since he came over here.' But she was not averse to adding insult to injury when she lied, 'Everyone knows! I was shocked when I realised that you were the only person who had no idea but I couldn't bring myself to tell you sooner. I didn't want to hurt you more than you've already been hurt, my poor darling,' and she softly caressed his cheek and victoriously pulled him gently towards her, cradling him against her softly beating bosom as she laughed inwardly. He was hers once again and the Blonde would want him more than ever if she thought she was losing him to someone else. Everything was falling neatly into place Andrea thought to herself. The years of planning had all been worthwhile and if Philip had looked into her eyes at that moment, he would have seen the vivid green change to a demonical black as she visualised her ultimate goal and congratulated herself on her ingenuity.

# Thirteen

Black Lomax looked out of the window onto the concrete way. It seemed sacrilege to have invited her here to their special place but he no longer cared. It was fool hardy of him as he could be recognised but he wanted to get the whole thing over before he backed out completely. It was only fair that she should be told, he supposed, but he hated confrontation and would do anything not to have one. In this case, there was no alternative.

He sat nervously chewing gum, inwardly rehearsing his lines, oblivious to his surroundings where customers sat obscured by pot plants while they talked in subdued voices. It was busy at this time of day as weary shoppers came in laden with expensive carrier bags, eager to rest their tired feet and have a drink. The aroma of freshly ground coffee which once smelt so sweet to him, seemed sour today and the raisin and pecan delicacies looked flat and unappetising as they reached towards the ceiling being piled so high on trays. He felt like running from the place to give himself time to think of some other way to do this but it was too late. Some movement attracted his attention. She came hurrying through the doorway, her coat blowing around in her rush, her face flushed and her eyes alight as she saw him. She looked amazing. It seemed that the whole interior had adopted a more vibrant atmosphere and for a moment he was tempted to delay the whole issue. She slipped easily into the chair opposite him, her graceful body folding underneath her effortlessly. He tried not to look into her eyes but he was beguiled by them. She removed her coat to reveal a fine, Cashmere top which clung to the curves of her body.

'Look, Andrea…' he started, hunting for the right words but she stopped him and leaned in towards him so that he could smell the sweetness of her body. She took his hand. His first instinct was to pull away, to repel any further intimacy between them, but he could not.

'Black, I had such an amazing time with you. It was like we were meant to be together!'

She moved closer to him and he could see the familiar curves of her breasts and he tried to erase the naked image of them.

'Andrea….' he started but she knew he was going to tell her about the Blonde and she could not bear to hear any of it.

'We are so good together…just like we were seven years ago!' She looked questioningly at him but there was no response. She was no longer the Andrea who had seduced Philip but, Andy, the teenager of years before.

'I love you, Black! I've never stopped loving you. I've waited all these years to be with you again.'

His resolve hardened. He had to put an end to this school girl infatuation. He realised the woman sitting opposite him was still a child with childish dreams.

'I've not been entirely honest with you, Andrea,' he said looking down to the fine grain of the table top and avoiding her eyes, 'There's been someone else all along. Someone I'm in love with. I should have told you at the outset, when we met again, but there never seemed to be the right opportunity.' She listened intently, 'You see, she's married and couldn't see me so often, then I bumped into you. I was lonely plus you are pretty irresistible!' He tried to lighten the situation.

They sat this way for a few moments, his dark eyes darting upwards as two customers passed their table. He lowered his voice even further so that only she could hear what he had to say, most of which she knew already.

'We're leaving for the States in a couple of weeks then she'll get a divorce and we'll get married.'

Married! Leaning back in her chair, she showed none of the terror she was feeling. Her face was painted with a tranquil smile. Once he had started confessing, Black found it difficult to stop.

'There was a time when I thought I'd have to forget her. I thought she didn't feel anything for me and loved her husband. I probably would have done if he hadn't found some other woman and left but then she changed in a way and I suppose I've caught her on the rebound or something but I don't care. I want her to come with me and we can start afresh.'

'Going back to the States?' she muttered almost inaudibly as she clasped and unclasped her hands while contemplating the failure of her plan to make the Blonde want Philip again.

'I don't know why I'm telling you all this. God knows, you would probably rather not hear it…but it sorta makes me feel better to come clean. I only wish I had told you sooner. This woman is what I've been looking for all my life. I feel secure and everything inexplicable with her. You do understand, Andrea?'

This couldn't be happening, she thought. Not to her—Andrea Winbech who had everything! He was all she had ever wanted since she was a teenager and she had spent all those years plotting, planning, yearning for this moment. She was older now and her father and mother could not do anything about it. She and Black could be together. Didn't he realise that!

He looked into her eyes and the smile left his lips. He felt sad that they should part like this, feeling guilty about the good times they had shared. It was like leaving an old friend…a buddy…but nothing else.

'I suppose I understand,' she lied, a faint smile flickering across her lips as she thought that he wasn't getting away with dumping her twice. 'It must have taken a lot for you to tell me this and I'm grateful.'

She was calmer now having known most of this information before but what shocked her was that she did not know that they planned to get married and go to the States together.

'You're so young, Andrea, so wonderfully young and alive. Someday you'll understand when it happens to you,' he said patronisingly. Her eyes filled with tears.

'You know it's happened to me!' she sobbed. He looked on anxiously as she allowed herself to weep openly. It was too much for him to endure and he pulled her towards him and gathered her in his arms, ignoring the puzzled stares of other customers.

'My poor Baby! Please don't cry. I wouldn't have had this happen for the world,' and he cradled her, stroking her hair, as though protecting her from the outside world. 'I'm sorry, so sorry,' he kept whispering to her as his lips brushed over the warm skin, wet with salty tears.

'Black…' she sobbed, 'would you do something for me?'

'Sure,' he replied with resolve, anything to stop her crying and making a scene.

'Can we see each other just one more time before you go? Not here…where everyone can see us but somewhere we can be alone, where we can talk? It would make it so much easier to take if we could.'

'Of course we can, Honey.' His mind was racing. He hadn't meant to make any promises but he supposed he owed her that much. Where was the harm in it if it meant things would be easier for her. 'Sure, Baby, we'll arrange something. Don't you worry now.' He dried her eyes with a tissue and coaxed her to smile again which she did having extracted his promise. She knew that he would keep it. All was not yet lost.

# Fourteen

Andrea Winbech let herself into her flat at Cambridge Mansions. She felt angry. Things weren't going her way and now she had to deal with Phillip. It was hard keeping up the pretence but it had to be done. She was hoping he would be gone soon.

When she entered the lounge, she nearly exploded. Empty cups of coffee, cans of beer and old newspapers littered the room and the place was in chaos. She hated untidiness. Couldn't he even clear up after himself? She had only been gone a short time and she had to put up with this and Phillip! As she stood looking at the mess, Phillip came in behind her.

'Hello, darling, I've been waiting for you to come back,' and he kissed her neck. She flinched slightly then remembered her plan and changed her facial expression immediately. She turned quickly to surprise him.

'Philip, I'm going to have a baby!' She stood motionless, her eyes animated with excitement. For a moment, he surveyed her face in silence until the words seeped into his brain.

'A baby?' he mumbled incredulously, as he sat down on the sofa, his body sinking into its softness.

'Yes, a baby! Sometime in May next year!'

He did not hear her last words but jumped from his seat, lifted her in his arms and spun her round and round again, their bodies clasped in unison for the crazy dance of happiness which gripped him. Then he looked at her and kissed her forehead and could not believe what he was hearing. He was deliriously happy but could not find words to express how he felt. It was what he had always dreamt of. A baby, a real baby, his baby.

'Well, say something…' Andrea prompted.

'I'm speechless. It's wonderful!' Philip said quietly.

Everything he had always wanted was coming to fruition. He had always yearned for children. His life would be incomplete without them but the Blonde had never shared his enthusiasm.

Here was his moment. Here was another woman telling him the words he longed to hear. He was about to become a father. It was unbelievable. He imagined tiny fingers gripping his hand, relying on him, looking to him for comfort and protection and he thought all the things expectant fathers think about. A new brilliance sneaked into his eyes.

'I've got to ask for a divorce,' he said suddenly interrupting his contemplation. He turned to the redhead who was smiling smugly. 'Don't you see? Now is the time. It's got to be.'

'There's no rush, Philip. Tomorrow will do!' she joked.

'No!' he said defiantly, 'Tonight will be even better and then we shall celebrate!'

Andrea applauded herself inwardly. Her plan was progressing better than she had anticipated. A baby and divorce would hopefully stop the Blonde from going to the States. She would be determined to get Philip back. He kissed her tenderly, put on his jacket and disappeared before she had time to say anything else.

Out in the cold night air, Philip strode to his car, a new bounce in his step, head buzzing with plans for the future and his forthcoming family. How his life had turned upside down in such a short while. He could hardly believe it was happening to him. Philip, who had never asked much out of life was now in the thick of it. A new wife, perhaps? No, definitely a new wife! Only a week or so ago he had contemplated seeing the Blonde, perhaps broaching the subject of their marriage and trying again and here he was, on his way to ask for a divorce!

But it was reasonable. Andrea was a wonderful girl and in a few years, he could see her surrounded by lovely children all with her red hair and beautiful soft skin. He found it peculiar though that she had never struck him as being the maternal type. It was just that she was so young, seemed so flighty at times that she did not give the impression of being the perfect mother. But possibly in a few years she would settle down in her ways and be content. He would help her. His age and experience would be useful to mould her for the task and together they would raise a family.

He drove as fast as he could through the traffic. It was rush hour and the roads were crowded with pedestrians straggling along the sidewalks bathed in the sheen of street lights, some taking the limelight as a passing car caught them in its headlights. He felt good. He wanted to shout to everyone about his good fortune but it could wait. There was plenty of time to let the rest of the world know about it. First, he had to tell the most important person. Yes, she was still important to him. If only it had been her telling him this news, then everything would have been perfect but life wasn't like that. Perhaps they could still be friends. Perhaps she would share his enthusiasm for his children and maybe visit them. No, it would never do. Life was just not like that. Feelings ran too deeply. He could not expect too much.

The entrance to his home looked unfamiliar. How easily he had shed his old surroundings and habits. Something about this thought frightened him. He had always imagined himself as a being bathed in tradition, someone who stuck to one road, never veering from his path in life. He thought of himself as an unexceptional character who would cruise through life contentedly. That was the word…contented. He was quietly successful with his work, never asking for the accolades like others did but aware that his associates had a deep respect for his talents. There were others who shone at the same craft, who claimed all the prizes and compliments, living in their own glory for a few months but he continued long after they had all fallen by the wayside. He had lasting quality, born from a childhood struggle to survive. And yet, here he was, about to ask the only woman he had ever loved, to divorce him because the girl he had so easily seduced in his office, was pregnant, about to make him a father and make his life complete. Where had his integrity gone? He was so confused. Deliriously happy yet miserable. He wondered where he had gone wrong and thought that perhaps he had not shed his former life after all.

He felt like a stranger at the same door which had welcomed him back not so long ago. He wondered if he should use his key but then thought it might be an invasion of her privacy, so he rang the bell and waited on the stone steps like a visitor. He knew she was at home as there were lights shining through the blinds from the lounge windows. She would answer soon. He only hoped that he was not with her. He couldn't bear that. He had to be alone with her.

Presently, the door opened just a little. Her face was pale and thin, much thinner than he remembered. She looked stressed but he thought it might just be tiredness. She wore a loose shift which hid the lines of her body making her look older. For a moment, he thought that it would be unwise to inflict more suffering on her because he still felt guilty about leaving the way he did. It was true that she had given him reason to leave but he could forgive her that. He was used to being compassionate and understanding. These feelings were as much a part of him as his need to breathe. Over the last few years these attributes had been diminished to a certain extent by his insecurity where love was concerned.

'Sorry to call without warning but this is rather urgent. Do you mind if I come in?' he asked apologetically.

'Of course not,' she said warmly and stood aside to let him pass. She knew it was not good policy to be so welcoming. The past had proved that to her but she could not help express how she was feeling. It was good to see him. She had been so lonely since he had left. Black could have stayed with her but that was not her way. Everyone had their place in the order of things and Black had no place in the life she had shared with Philip.

She had waited for this moment but as time went by she despaired of it ever materialising. Deep inside her she knew that he would come back and hoped that they could try again, forget what had happened and here he was, standing in front of her, his eyes more animated than ever. He looked young again, like a teenager. Here was the Philip she met and fell in love with.

'The fire's on in the lounge. Shall we go in there?' she asked, feeling rather clumsy not knowing what to say to him.

He followed her into the familiar lounge. It looked dull and lifeless. He had never noticed this before. It had always been the same, something solid and he had never thought to question any of it. The glow from the fire tended to emphasise the dreariness of its surroundings. She sat on the sofa and it was as if nothing had changed and nothing had happened to them as he sat opposite on the chair he always used.

'I don't really know how to put this…' He said clasping and unclasping his hands, elbows resting on the arms of the chair. He was different, she thought, happier, more at ease, less tense than he had been before he moved out. She wished she had been responsible for this change but she was not. She presumed it was someone else and she was right. 'I told you I'd met this girl? Well…I'm going to be a father!'

His face lit up for an instant as he wanted her to share his excitement but was stopped by the look of horror and disbelief on her face. She did not speak but stared at him. It was a shock. She tried to say something, tried to control herself but her pride would not allow her to show the hurt she was feeling. She felt she had driven him to this. She had made it happen and the Blonde realised that she only had herself to blame. Hatred for herself as well as Andrea, rose within her. She tried to hold back tears.

'I can't believe it! It can't be true!'

'I'm sorry,' Philip whispered, 'I had to tell you.'

'How could you?' she screamed.

He tried to calm her.

'You understand, don't you?'

'Understand?' she kept repeating, 'You want me to understand!'

He moved over to the sofa and sat beside her. She wanted to scream and shout, to give vent to her feelings but all she could do was tremble. He tried to put his arm round her shoulder.

'Leave me alone,' she shouted and pushed him away. 'Just leave me alone! Don't touch me! I don't want you to touch me!'

'I'm sorry,' he said weakly and drew away. He had not expected this reaction. Had he only been thinking of his own feelings? Having gone this far he had to continue.

'I know this is not the right time to discuss this...but I want a divorce!'

'A divorce?' she asked incredulously.

'Yes. It's got to be settled soon. I want to marry Andrea!'

The Blonde felt destroyed having nowhere to turn. She sighed and lay back on the sofa, her head pounding. She could hardly absorb all that he was saying and felt numb. They sat in silence for a while then she said flatly, 'How did this happen to us, Phillip?'

He stood up and put his hands in his pocket and looked at the floor.

'You know what happened...' And he looked up with watery eyes, remembering the hurt and forgetting for a moment, his excitement.

'If you want a divorce, then go ahead! Why should I stop you,' the Blonde uttered quietly not looking at him. He moved towards the door then turned back.

'I can't leave you like this. Can I get you something… A drink, anything?' he asked concerned.

'No thank you,' she said, staring into her own future while he stood, hands in pockets, shoulders stiff.

'Well…if you're sure…I'll go now.' and he left silently, his mood much heavier than when he arrived.

The Blonde was left alone to consider her life. She had not meant things to turn out like this and she thought back to the evening when she had first met Black. It seemed so long ago that their eyes had met and they exchanged their first few words. It had happened because of her boredom and Philip's wish for her to stay at home and start a family. She didn't want her independence to be taken from her but if she could have seen the consequences of her actions, she would never have allowed it to happen.

# Fifteen

The days passed quickly after Philip asked for a divorce. The view from the lounge window was basically the same as it had always been but, as the Blonde stood studying it, she felt that it ought to have changed drastically. Everything else in her life was undergoing a transition. She found little comfort as she looked from the window, dusk falling over the city, a hint of red amber tinging the horizon of the late afternoon scene. It would soon be mid-winter, a time when she had cossetted herself in her home, gathering those things around her which would give her the most solace throughout the long, cold winter evenings. It was a time for hibernation and she used it mentally and physically to renew herself for the world of the summer when she became alive again. Yet she enjoyed winter as much as summer because she could curl up in front of the fire with Philip, sit in the darkness watching the flames devour the logs. It was a time for sharing each other's thoughts and hopes but last winter had wrenched them apart.

Philip had expressed his desire to have a family and she remembered the feeling of being trapped as he pressed her to make a decision. It had spoiled the whole atmosphere but what faced her this winter? There would be no more of those comforting evenings by the fire. They were a thing of the past.

If he had never told her about the baby, she was prepared to win him back. Even though she loved Black, she was scared of a new future and felt safe with Philip. But his admission had changed everything and made it easy for her to make a decision.

She thought about Black. He was her passion. How long do passions last before they disintegrate into something else? Still, it would not be long before she flew off from this life and out to a new one. She was neither excited nor afraid of the prospect as her recent experiences had drained all feeling from her. She had changed lately and could feel the changes taking place within her. A new calm occupied her body as she faced life alone without Philip. Now she was mistress of her own destiny and felt renewed confidence in her own ability to choose.

The Blonde and Black had spent a lot of time together in the last few weeks. There was nothing to stop them seeing each other and sometimes she would stay over at his place for a few days before feeling the need to be alone. Then came the time when there were only a few days left before they flew to the States. She had seen Philip and told him of her plans and she remembered how silently he had taken the news. He never spoke or looked at her for a long time as he deliberated her words. Philip did not want her to leave. There was something incredibly final about her going. She had been his life for so long. He had hoped that she would always be around, near enough for him to have some contact but the States were so far away.

She waited patiently looking over the darkening sky. Eventually, the doorbell rang and she eagerly ran to answer it. Engulfed in his arms, she felt the chill on his coat from the descending night air but she nestled in close to him and responded as his cold lips sought hers. He was her anchor now.

'Hey, Kitten, save some of this for America! I hope you'll have plenty of time to spoil me when we hit the States!' and he laughed as he looked into her eyes. She returned his smile and holding him by the hand, walked him into the lounge.

'I'm sorry I've been so busy lately, Honey, but I've had so many loose ends to tie up before we go. I don't intend coming back here for some time,' he said drawing her towards him and kissing her tenderly, 'I hope you don't intend to come back except for a visit,' he added, almost enquiringly as she gazed into his eyes.

'I don't intend to!'

'Good! Then that's settled.' It seemed to reassure him. 'Hey, I've got plans for us when we arrive. As soon as Philip gets this divorce sorted, we can get married. I've been working the whole thing out. You're gonna get one hell of a wedding, Babe! I feel so damn lucky! You're the best thing that's ever happened to me!'

The Blonde tucked her head into his chest and burrowed into the warmth of his body. She liked listening to him talk this way, planning their future. It gave her life some purpose but she could not share his enthusiasm to the same extent as an invisible string still attached her to Philip and Black was stretching it to the limit. Then she reasoned with herself. Philip had planned his life regardless of her so why shouldn't she do the same.

'Look, Honey,' Black broke into her thoughts, 'I've got some business to finish off this weekend while you're seeing Leonie.' His conscience badgered him for deceiving her but it had to be done. 'It will give you a chance to see her on your own before we fly off next week. I'd only be in the way. I'll pick you up from there on Sunday and we can drive back together. Does that sound OK?'

It made sense. She wanted to be alone with Leonie before she left and this would be her last opportunity.

'Of course. We'll have a lot to talk about and you'll only get bored!' she said.

'Good!' He kissed her forehead and asked, 'Are you happy?'

'Of course I'm happy!' and she felt that she was despite all her misgivings.

'Let's get you down to the station for your train. Is Leonie collecting you at the other end?'

'Yes,' she said as she collected her case and gave it to Black. She took a last look round the hallway and her eyes strayed up the staircase of her home. Soon she would have to leave for good and her heart felt heavy. Black closed the door behind them and, with a protective arm round her shoulder, steered her towards his car.

As her train slowed into the suburban station, the Blonde studied the faces on the platform searching for Leonie. She saw her and Leonie started to walk towards the train as it came to a halt. She hardly recognised her sister. Leonie had a new hair style, a short cut and her natural colour of dark brown had gold highlights which gave her a more youthful look. They hugged each other.

'Let me look at you!' the Blonde cried holding Leonie at arm's length. 'You look amazing!'

Leonie smiled broadly.

'It's only a new haircut!' she laughed, 'I've been meaning to have a change for years but never had the courage. Now I feel I can do anything.'

Arms around each other's waists, they walked to her car like two chatty teenagers.

'But you've got a whole new style!' the Blonde said. 'New clothes, boots, bag. A whole new you!'

'Yes, a new me!' Leonie giggled and they hugged each other closer.

It had been a while since she had seen Leonie. She had made a good recovery at home and now she definitely seemed in charge of her life. Her eyes were radiant. Gone were the stress lines and red rimmed eyes from crying. She looked so healthy and full of energy.

They chatted on the drive home and Leonie had a permanent smile on her lips.

'You must tell me your secret,' the Blonde teased. 'You look so young.'

'Well, actually,' Leonie started, 'It's not entirely down to my new image!' She hesitated for a moment as though she were about to divulge a huge secret. 'Do you remember Richard Browning? He was a bit older than me and used to go to that Boys' School up the road from us. You remember? We used to meet his crowd in the Café on a Friday night?'

'Vaguely,' the Blonde replied.

'Well, I joined this Bridge Club after I threw Jeff out. I needed something to occupy my mind and Annie, next door, said she would babysit so off I went and who should be there but Richard! He recognised me straight away and we got chatting. He's been divorced for a few years now and so we arranged to meet again. We've been for dinner a few times and to the theatre. He's great company.' She carefully steered the car round the country bends as she spoke.

'Good for you. I'm so pleased for you. You don't know how happy it makes me feel to know that you are in a good place, especially now that I'm off to the States.'

They drove through avenues of houses, some quaint, others large and imposing as the architecture changed. Soon they were in Leonie's drive and Jeff stood at the door to welcome them. Leonie sniffed disapprovingly.

'He's only here to see you before you go and to see the children,' she explained.

The Blonde felt awkward, unsure how she should approach Jeff. He looked ill. Thin, haggard and unkempt. His blue eyes, once so vibrant, now looked dull and lifeless. He had aged so much. She moved towards him and kissed his cheeks, her usual greeting of all the years that had gone before. A warm look came into his dead eyes for an instant and there was a glimmer of a smile.

'It's great to see you,' he said, holding her for a moment and she could feel his bony skeleton pressing through his clothes. He ushered her indoors behind Leonie and they sat in the kitchen. Before she had time to ask how he was, he started to explain his appearance. 'I've been off work for a few months now. In fact, I'm handing in my resignation soon. Can't face work any longer!'

The Blonde was shocked.

'Oh, you mustn't do that, Jeff! You're such a good designer, it would be such a loss.'

He wrung his scrawny hands together and looked at the floor. She noticed the deep lines etched into his face. They hadn't been there before.

'I'm destroyed! I've had it! I'm finished now!' he cried and the Blonde hardly recognised this person who was once so confident and charming. Apart from his physical appearance, she could see that he was heading for a breakdown. Leonie put cups of coffee in front of them.

'He's not eating and drinking far too much,' she said with indifference. 'I keep telling him but he won't listen!'

He looked at her with watery eyes, his feet tapping constantly on the ground, his hands never still.

'She's right,' he said lamely, 'but I can't do anything about it. I've got nothing left but booze. I'm staying up in the cottage in Norfolk but it's to be sold soon so I don't know what I'm going to do. It's so lonely up there. All I can do is drink. The doctor's given me pills but I don't think they work if you drink as well.'

Leonie frowned at him.

'Pathetic! I've told you often enough!'

The Blonde thought that Leonie was enjoying Jeff's distress. She was now in control and he was suffering. He turned away from her towards the Blonde.

'How are you?' he said quietly, looking at the floor. 'Are you happy about leaving Philip and going to the States?'

She wasn't expecting to be faced with such a question and was glad when they were interrupted by the arrival of the children who had been playing upstairs. They ran to her in one large bundle of excitement, jumping on her knee and putting their little arms round her neck.

'Auntie! How long are you staying? Can you read me a story? Can you play with my train set?'

The questions all came at once until Leonie intervened.

'It's nearly bedtime, kids, so a quick story and then you can see Auntie tomorrow. Daddy will take you up and read to you.'

Jeff led them away, a doleful look on his face as he noted his new position in the family.

Later, when the children were asleep, Jeff returned and all three sat by the log burner having a celebratory drink for the Blonde.

'We were sorry to hear that you and Philip had split,' Leonie started, 'Is there a chance you might get back together? Of course, it's no business of ours... perhaps you don't even want to speak about it...?'

The Blonde knew that Leonie did not know the whole story. She looked into the firelight and prepared herself.

'It's alright. I don't mind talking about it now. I haven't had anyone to talk to so it's nice to share it.' She shrugged her shoulders. 'It's maybe a bit too late to talk about a reconciliation. After all, she's pregnant and that's what Philip always wanted... to be a father.' She looked at Leonie's shocked face. 'He could hardly leave her in that condition, even if he wanted to...and he doesn't!'

'I didn't realise,' Leonie said, looking into her glass and swirling it round in her hand so that the clear liquid clung to the sides, 'But how do you feel about the whole thing?'

'I'm afraid to think about it at the moment. I've made my decision to go to the States with Black and I can't think any further than that. It's too much to handle, everything happening at once. I thought that Philip would come back, it was only a question of time and by being on my own for a while I thought I'd be able to sort out what I felt for him and

Black. And he did come back…to tell me she was pregnant and to ask for a divorce!'

Leonie and Jeff looked at each other, both thinking different thoughts.

'Where did Philip meet this woman?' asked Leonie.

'I'm not sure. I don't know anything about her except that she exists. I found her name and address written on a piece of paper in Philip's pocket. Andrea something…Windersberg or something like that,' and she drained her glass.

A horrifying silence descended on the little group and the Blonde looked up to see Leonie's incredulous expression change to anger while Jeff turned ashen and jumped up from his chair, his drink shaking in his hand.

'Christ, I don't believe it! It can't be true!' Jeff said with disbelief while he supported himself against the fireplace.

'Andrea Winbech?' screeched Leonie, her voice rising.

'Yes, that's the name,' said the Blonde, 'What's wrong?'

Leonie ignored her question.

'Well, well…Andrea Winbech again! I can't believe it! She must have a thing about our family!' Leonie said with malice. She poured a large gin into her glass. 'What the hell does she want? Can't she find a man who isn't married and who's nearer her own age? Or is that the attraction?'

She flopped onto her chair. The name brought back all the trauma of the last year for Leonie and Jeff but from different angles. Leonie relived the collapse of her marriage and the dark despair of the months following her attempted suicide. Jeff pictured Andrea for an instant and the yearnings he had to suppress after she left resurfaced momentarily before reminding him that, between them, they had destroyed everything he valued.

'She wants something she can't have then tires of it… unless…' he sighed.

'Unless what?' urged the Blonde, the horrible realisation showing in her eyes.

'Unless she has an ulterior motive?' He sat down wearily, holding his empty glass in both hands, his elbows supported on his knees. 'Why Philip?' He could not ignore the grain of jealousy which crept into his mind.

'Oh, my god…' said the Blonde thinking of Philip.

'There must be more to it than that,' Jeff said although he was finding it difficult to talk about her and Leonie was finding it difficult to listen. 'She's not the type to settle down to family life unless she's changed drastically.' He sighed and avoided Leonie's gaze. 'I mean…I thought it would be the last thing she would want. Unless…' Something seemed to click in his mind, fall into place as memories of Andrea came creeping into his consciousness, giving him a sickening feeling in his stomach, '…unless she wanted something else and this was the only way she could get it.'

'But what?' asked the Blonde, 'She's got Philip, hasn't she? She's got what she wants!'

Jeff sighed deeply.

'Let's not spoil our time together thinking about her. Philip has made his decision. Let's hope things work out for everyone.'

They changed the conversation yet all three had time to think and the name 'Andrea' was never far from their thoughts. She had crept into their lives like a plague and had left a trail of devastation behind her.

# Sixteen

Philip followed her into the bedroom. It was dimly lit, the available light casting a sombre hue over the space.

'But why do you have to go away this weekend of all weekends?' he pleaded. Ignoring him, she started packing her small case. First, she opened the wardrobe which housed her vast array of clothes and, without stopping to choose which she should wear, pulled a flimsy dress from a hanger, almost ripping the material in her hurry. 'You should be with me at a time like this! Surely it's only natural,' he said, trying to appear in her line of vision as she moved from one side of the room to the other, opening drawers and collecting her possessions before throwing them into the case. He did not want to pressurise her knowing how sensitive she could be. Lately, her moods had been so changeable and unnatural but he thought this was because of the pregnancy. At times, he was finding it difficult to cope with her temperament but assumed it was all caused by her hormones and thought he would just have to be more patient and understanding.

Suddenly, she stopped her frenetic packing and looked him fully in the eyes.

'Philip, you don't seem to understand,' she said defiantly, 'I'm not coming back! This time next week I'll be on the other side of the world!' and she threw a pair of sandals on top of her untidily packed clothes and clicked the case shut as though she were closing a chapter in her life.

'But…I don't…understand,' Philip stammered as he tried to put his arm round her, 'You're going to have my baby! You can't just leave!'

She pushed him away.

'Oh, can't I!' she screamed, turning round quickly, her long hair lashing against her face before it came to rest on her shoulders. 'Just watch me! I can do anything I like and you can't stop me!'

He took a step towards her, his fear turning to anger. Grabbing her slim arm, he held it tightly preventing her from leaving the room. She looked down at his hand, the tight grip burning into her skin and, with eyes blazing, a renewed haughtiness in her manner, said, 'Go on! Try to stop me! If all else fails, use force!'

As she spat the words into his face, it slowly dawned on Philip that the vixen had been using him. He had been vulnerable and had fallen for her clever manipulations to achieve her own objectives. He had no idea what these were and now he did not care. All he cared about was his unborn child but even that would be a part of her. Finally realising his mistake, he felt sick. What a fool he had been not to see all this earlier.

She buttoned her jacket, tossing the long strands of flaming auburn hair out behind her as she adjusted the collar. A final look in the mirror to check her appearance then she picked up her case, making her way to the door.

'What will you do with the baby?' he asked almost inaudibly as she laid down her case and turned to him, hands thrust deeply into her pockets. Gone was the soft Andrea who pampered him, saw to his every wish. Gone too was the tigress who scolded and bullied him into asking for a divorce. Her mask had dropped and he stood looking at her as she really was. She was a devil. Her green eyes blazed with demonic determination. A fear gripped his soul. Their life together had been a sham.

'You poor, simpering idiot,' she said through clenched teeth, 'Now you can return to your wife which is what you've always wanted to do anyway and, thanks to me, she'll be delighted to see you. The thought of divorce and maybe losing you, might make her want you more, poor cow!' She lifted her case, and almost as an afterthought, a peculiar grin spreading over her mouth said, 'I told you I was pregnant but I didn't say it was yours... did I?' Philip couldn't speak. He was paralysed with disbelief. 'Put the key through the letter box when you leave.'

In a single moment, she had shattered his world. Everything he was looking forward to, his new future, had gone. From being feverishly happy one week, he found himself sinking into despair. There was no baby, no pregnancy. It had all been a horrible lie. She needed to hurt, to see someone hurt as she had been hurt.

The door closed behind her leaving Philip alone. She never looked back. No word of pity or regret issued from her lips. These were the cold, hard facts. He felt like a fool. She was right. He had been a bloody fool.

Left alone in the cavernous apartment, Philip paced round the room trying to make sense of the last hour. He felt he had been washed out to sea and there was no way back. This place was not his home yet he had forfeited his right to stay in his real home.

He thought about the Blonde and what he had lost. He wondered if she would ever take him back or indeed if she still wanted him. He thought about Andrea and how manipulative she had been. If the baby wasn't his, then whose was it? She had destroyed all his aspirations for the future and the light from the window turned from grey to black as the night sky enveloped the flat in darkness. Philip lay on the sofa and wept. Just as she had appeared so suddenly in his life, she had left, and Philip never saw Andrea Winbech again.

Black Lomax studied himself in the mirror while smoothing down his thick, black hair with a comb. He was slightly irritated that he had to go through with this fiasco because he had made a promise. He scolded himself for being so weak. What did they have to say to each other? He cursed himself for being so indulgent where women were concerned and resolved never to allow this situation to recur. Next week he would be back home. There would only be one woman in his life and his intention was to keep it that way. But he was a prisoner of his masculine weaknesses and felt he owed it to Andrea to see her once again as she had asked. She had always been available when he had wanted her so it was not too much to give one evening of his life in return.

He smoothed the collar of the expensive white jacket and stroked the well-cut lines with his fingers. For a moment, he checked himself in the mirror. He was pleased that the last month of strain did not show in his face. He had so many things on his mind, he could do without this journey but it would only be a night. He would not allow her to keep him any longer, no matter how she tried to persuade him by turning those devilishly wicked eyes on him.

He felt guilty not having told the Blonde the truth about this. He felt ashamed. He ought to have told her. What difference would it have made? They had a whole lifetime ahead of them but it was too late now. He would tell her later. Explain the whole thing.

Black quickly collected his car keys and throwing an overnight bag in the back, raced off into the busy traffic, his tyres screeching. He weaved in and out of the lanes as he was already late, probably because of his reluctance to go through with the evening.

As he waited for the lights to turn green, his fingers tapped an unknown rhythm on the steering wheel, releasing some of his anxiety. Perhaps she would not be there. Perhaps she would have changed her mind, having seen the futility of meeting for the last time. These thoughts raced through his mind as he pushed the car into first gear and drove its sleek lines at speed ahead of the other waiting vehicles. He wanted to be anywhere but here. He wanted to say goodbye to those people he would miss, wanted to spend some time with the gang from the studios but he supposed it could wait until tomorrow…tomorrow when all this would be behind him.

He came to a halt outside the arranged meeting place and his eyes searched the faces of the hundreds of people who spewed forth from the tube exit but he could not see her. Hoping she had changed her mind, he was about to drive away from the kerb when someone tapped on his windscreen. She had found him.

'Hi,' she said as he rolled the window down. He tried to hide his disappointment.

'I had a coffee across the road since you hadn't arrived. I saw you from the there.' She nodded in the direction of a small Bistro, its wall dull and grey amongst the other buildings, its shades dirty and weathered by the dust and soot. It mirrored how he felt.

'I'm sorry. I couldn't make it any sooner,' he said, throwing her case in the back beside his.

'Well, you're here now,' she smiled, 'and that's all that matters.'

She gave him a proprietary glance and Black's mood plummeted even further. He was beginning to hate her for having walked back into his life again and he despised himself for allowing it to happen just when things were starting to crystalise in his life.

He drove away with a great screech of his tyres, anger building within him as he sped through the traffic, regardless of caution. Soon they were out on the open road, leaving the city behind and with it, the grimy buildings which looked morbid and depressing in the light of the falling dusk. Fields began to take their place and the countryside opened up around them revealing its brown winter colours, cooler pictures of what had been. Black felt despondent when he thought back to summer with the Blonde when the field had been a glorious yellow and life felt good.

# Seventeen

Two tired figures walked wearily by the hedgerow of the field which was once yellow. Their crumpled, worn jackets hung like sacks on their bodies, belying the men's years. On their heads, they wore caps, thick with the dust and grime of past weeks on the fields. Their collarless shirts, once white, had turned to grey with constant washing, being stained with sweat, mud and toil. Their weathered faces spoke of the past summer's work in the fields when the world around them was an open book which they wrote upon at their leisure, of simple things which were meaningful to them. It had been a good year and they felt proud of their work. In their isolation they had contributed so much even though their bones ached and their backs reached breaking point at times. They were proud men and this pride held them up when faced with difficulties.

They walked in silence through the darkening evening light, picking their way along the verge of the narrow road, brushing against thorny hedges thickening with berries. They looked simultaneously behind them as they heard the purr of a car engine in the distance. The repetitive noise increased gradually until it was nearly upon them. They stopped together and watched the car wind its way from the horizon like an angry crocodile weaving through the waters of a calm river. Eventually it drew level, the noise of its powerful engine full volume as it passed, causing the grass around them to flatten then right itself. It was not the type of car normally seen in their area and they recognised it immediately. They listened as the sound of the motor waned and it disappeared from sight round a bend in the road.

'It's 'im again,' one said to the other, nodding in the direction the car had taken. 'sept this time, he's got a different one! Pity, I was getting' to like t'other!'

They laughed together at the shared joke.

'Yeah, but did you see 'er face! She looked mad! She b screamin' at 'im! Poor bloke 'ad 'is window open, probably trying to get away from 'er!'

They laughed again.

'But did you see 'er eyes?' the younger man asked, 'She's got the Devil in 'em!' and his face took on a serious expression as he looked at his companion for a reaction.

'Now, Thomas, you outta not be thinkin' about things like that!' and he walked on.


'Black,' Andrea said softly as they left the city behind. 'Take me with you to the States!'

It was like a bombshell. He slowed his driving to look at her face to see if it was a joke but all he saw was wilful determination. Surely, she couldn't be serious. He gripped the steering wheel tightly, his knuckles white as he resumed his normal speed.

'Take you with me?' he asked incredulously. 'But Andrea…I thought I explained.'

'I know what you explained and I also know this woman. You think you're in love with her but it's no good, Black, she's still in love with her husband,' she said stonily.

'What do you mean? What can you know about her?' he asked dryly.

'Everything! I know everything I need to know about her,' she replied. 'You see, over the past months I've looked into her mind for one reason and I even know how she thinks.'

She sat back looking slightly smug and very confident. Black looked ahead. He was confused. Curse her, he thought. Why did I ever agree to see her again? I should have known that someone so tempting, so beautiful, could not be for real. There had to be something more to her and now I'm cornered, caught in a trap. He searched his mind, frantically trying to find an escape. He clawed at the outer limits of his consciousness but the search was futile. There was no escape.

'I...I don't understand your meaning,' he said, trying to give himself time to think.

'It's quite simple, Black, darling.' Her use of the intimate word made beads of perspiration form on his forehead and a nauseous feeling began to choke him. 'Ever since I met you, all those years ago, there hasn't been anyone else for me. Not a day passed when I did not think about you or vow that I would make sure we would be together again, just like we were then. Everything I've done has been for you. When you stopped writing, it did not stop me from planning ahead. I knew that one day you would want me again and so my life was consumed by learning how to be the perfect specimen. I even had a part in securing your contract with the Television Company, through my father, of course. He didn't connect you, the big star, with that boy of long ago!' and she added with distaste, 'For once I found he had a use!' She continued more lightly now, snuggling close to him and looking up into his eyes which were focussed on the road ahead. 'I even asked my father to find me a position in the Studios just so I could be close to you. It was no problem…he has plenty of contacts and was glad to see me doing something useful for a change. So you see, it wasn't really Fate which brought us together again…it was me…because I love you so much.'

Black felt sick. He pushed her away with his arm.

'Don't be like that, Black, please don't!' and she continued to move closer to him. 'At first, it was enough just to see you from a distance but, of course, it couldn't stay like that, not after what we shared all those years ago…not after all the planning I'd done. I've remembered that summer so vividly. I never forgot you. I cried after I had to leave you. I started to hate my father then…and my mother. But as time passed, I realised that nothing is ever final. Something can always be done if you want it enough.' Black visualised Winston Elliot Winbech berating her for seeing him and his features hardened. 'I waited for your letters but they never came. I was prepared to wait but only for so long and then I had to do something about it. You understand, don't you, Black?'

She held his arm making driving difficult. Black was angry. He was angry with her and angry with himself.

'But this is nonsense! How could you carry those feelings around for all those years? It was seven years ago, Andrea! A lot has happened since then. People change…'

'Eight!' she interrupted. 'Nearly eight. Eight long years since I lost my baby!'

'Baby?' Black screamed, 'What baby?'

'Your baby! I was pregnant when you left and they wouldn't allow me to keep it. The scandal would have been too great. I hated them but I needed them. You never contacted me and my letters came back unopened but I never stopped loving you. My feelings for you grew over those years and it's been worth everything to be here with you now.'

'But…a baby…?' Black's mouth was dry and he was having difficulty concentrating on the road. He felt sick. This was his worst nightmare.

'Yes, your baby!' Black swallowed hard. He could hardly believe what she was saying but it could be true. 'You don't realise what I've had to do. I knew as soon as I came over from the States that you were involved with that woman.' For a second, he turned to look at her with disgust. 'I had to do something drastic. I started an affair with her brother-in-law, Jeff. I made a tiny bit of a mistake as I thought he was her husband. However, it gave me an insight into her marriage. You were seeing more and more of her and her husband never suspected. I knew she was bored with their life. I could tell just by looking at her. Eventually, I took her husband away so that she would appreciate him more. Her pride would be hurt by the competition and she would eventually return to him, leaving the road open for me. She said she would move to the States with you but that was only a temporary decision. At the time, she had no alternative. But she won't do it. Black!'

Black's hands gripped the wheel tighter. He felt trapped. He hated her and hated what he was hearing.

'It's not true! We are going to the States, both of us! She wants to go! She loves me!' and he banged the steering wheel with his hands.

'She thinks she loves you but will she finally leave the husband she's been pining after since you've known her? Come on, Black! Be realistic!' she cried, her eyes blazing, willing him to oppose her. He said nothing. 'What has she done for you? What is she to you? Look what I've done for you! I've waited and waited, willing to take second place. You must know what we've been to each other. You can't deny it, Black!' she screamed at him with fanatical zest. Black suddenly realised how dangerous Andrea was. He could feel her madness yet he could not subdue his own anger.

'No!' he shouted, 'It's not true!' You mean absolutely nothing to me! Nothing!' and he spat the words in her direction. She was undeterred.

'Then why did you come this evening?' and he thought to himself, because I'm an honest, stupid, sentimental fool.

'There's something else I must tell you, Black.'

He ignored her knowing that she was willing him to look into her eyes just once. 'I'm expecting your baby and this time, I'm going to have it!'

She had finally slapped him in the face, killing his pride and self-respect. Gripping the wheel hard, he negotiated the winding road narrowly missing two farm workers walking by the wayside. How he wished he could swap places with one of them. The evening was becoming a nightmare.

'It...can't be! Not you! Not my...baby!' and he felt his whole life spin out of control. This was not the moment he had envisaged to be told of fatherhood and this was not the woman. He felt he was going insane.

'So you see, you'll have to take me to the States. After all, it would never do for a person in your position...in the public eye…think about the scandal, think about your career. But still, we can have a wonderful life…just the three of us!'

Her voice had turned sour, eating into his soul. He thought fleetingly about the Blonde and how it would be with them in the future. It was not true what Andrea had said about her. The Blonde loved him and she was going with him. Wasn't that enough? He would be there waiting at the airport for her and they would look back on this episode one day and laugh about it while gratuitously thinking about Andrea. 'Poor kid, so young, so disillusioned.' Perhaps they would wonder what happened to her and sit in their cushioned togetherness, untouched by her plight, glad to be rid of her encumbrance as they lived out their dreams. But the baby? What about the baby? He could not stand for this. It was too much getting pregnant to catch him and using an innocent life as bait. He tried to calm himself and took a deep breath before speaking. He had to be strong.

'Andrea, I have no intention of taking you to the States, baby or no baby! As far as I'm concerned, you were a welcome diversion from my confused life and helped me realise even more, that I'm in love with the Blonde. I have that to thank you for.' He felt bad saying this as it wasn't in his nature to be unkind. 'All those years ago I suppose you were the innocent child and I was no more than a kid myself…but it meant very little. We were so young. It was a nice memory of a hot summer but no more. Do you understand what I'm trying to say?'

He turned to her momentarily and was shocked to see the contorted expression on her face. It was an embodiment of everything evil and he averted his gaze. He couldn't understand what it meant and he shuddered when he realised what his words had done to her.

'No! No! No!' she screamed as her hands covered her eyes. Her fists clenched as she screwed up the once beautiful face into an unrecognisable mask. She shook with anger and hatred. 'I won't let you go…!'

And she lunged towards him and wrenched the steering wheel from his hands with all her Demonic strength, heaving it from him. For a moment, he was stunned then his reaction was to right it but it was too late. Ahead of them loomed the tree, its size and strength hitting them full force after the car veered in its direction, Black powerless to stop its progress. He slammed his feet on the brakes. A sickening thud was heard as the headlights zoomed in on the weathered bark of its great surface and then only darkness. All was silent except for the sizzle of the broken lights and the tinkle of glass as it fell in shattered pieces to the ground.

'Did 'e hear that?' The men looked at each other and then started to run. Faster and faster their muscular legs strode along the road, their jackets blowing out beside them in their haste. The crash had broken the silence of the evening and they knew that it could only be the car of the familiar figure they had seen driving this road many times before. Their hearts beat faster as their legs pounded the road surface.

The younger of the two men arrived at the tree first. Half Way Tree it was called, a spot known throughout the district for its picturesque views over the surrounding countryside. No one could remember when it had first been called this name but it became a landmark as it thrust its monster body out of the ground. Hundreds of years had passed it by and yet it stood majestically surveying the panoramic view. And now a tangled mass of crumpled metal lay at the base of its great trunk. A deep moaning, almost weeping emerged from the remnants of the vehicle. In the darkness which had engulfed the day, the young man searched in his pocket and pulled out a small box of matches. His hands were shaking as he struck one which immediately extinguished itself. He found another, hands trembling as he shielded its light from the rising breeze.

'O'er here, Will!' he shouted as the older man joined him from the depths of the murky evening. 'I can see 'er!'

He pulled at the door as the light from the match died leaving them alone in the eerie night. It gave without much effort and she lay slumped in front of him. Her head lay on the back of the seat, her red hair falling in folds over her shoulder. Blood trickled from her mouth in little, silent rivulets which ran downwards onto her jacket. She looked at peace, just as though she were sleeping. The older man pushed his friend aside.

''Ere, let me see! I've found the torch,' and he shone it on the white face while searching for her arm. His callous, grimy hands held her smooth wrist. 'Ain't no pulse there. Broke 'er neck, probably.'

The younger man pressed close behind him, looking over in horror at the apparition.

'I told 'ee she had the eyes o' the Devil, didn't I?'

'Don't fret, son! She ain't got no eyes for nuttin' now!' and he shook his head as he shone the torch further round the mangled wreck. 'Look! He's moanin'. Let's try gettin' him out!'

They ran round to where Black lay and pulled at the door, wrenching off the handle as they did so but entry evaded them. The back door lay at an angle, squashed in the middle but they worked with their hands, pulling and pushing, using any bits of metal they could find as levers. Using brute strength, eventually the door opened and the younger man climbed into the body of the car to where Black lay.

'Don't 'ee worry. We'll get 'ee out o' 'ere,' he said, comfortingly to the crumpled figure, his face a mass of blood, his legs helplessly caught below the body of the engine and the steering wheel sickeningly angled towards his ribs. There were faint sounds coming from his once large frame and the man, even in his horror of the blood soaked victim, tried to make sense of them. He turned to his companion on the outside.

''Es still alive but 'e's caught under the wheel. We'll 'ave to get an ambulance an' someone to cut 'im free.'

''Ere, let me 'av a look,' the older man said impatiently, pulling his friend out before hoisting himself forward to where Black was positioned. He too could hear the faint mutterings coming from him. He put his ear close beside the blood covered face, now unrecognisable as Black Lomax, Hollywood star, and listened carefully.

'Tell her…tell her it's…not true,' the voice said, almost inaudibly as he gasped for breath in between words. 'Tell her…I love her…I didn't…want this.'

The older man listened then tried to offer some comfort and said in a soft voice.

'I'll tell her. I'll make sure I tell her.'

He felt in the darkness for the wrist of the man he knew well from a distance. He found it enclosed in the sleeve of the blood soaked suit. It felt wet and warm and the pulse was very weak. Almost as soon as he found it and waited, hoping to feel a rhythmic beat, it suddenly stopped, quietly at first then faded to nothing and he realised that he was holding the wrist of a dead man.

# Eighteen

Leonie and the Blonde spent the weekend together. A familiar joy fell between them like an invisible piece of elastic which drew them together again. They spent time comfortably involved in looking through old photograph albums and reminiscing about their childhood and teenage years. They laughed like young girls as they brought the past to life for a few hours.

'Do you remember those two boys we met from Aske's School?' Leonie smiled. The Blonde shook her head. 'Remember, you liked the dark haired one and I liked the blonde but when we met up one Saturday the blonde one made a bee line for you and the dark haired one fancied me!' They laughed.

'I vaguely remember,' sighed the Blonde then she chuckled. 'Didn't we tell them that we had to go into Marks & Spencer's and they waited outside then we darted out the back door of the shop and never saw them again!' They laughed together. 'We never stopped running until we reached the Esplanade. We were out of breath and couldn't stop laughing!'

'How bad were we! Terrible teenagers! How could we do that to them? Anyway, you were the instigator!'

'No I wasn't! You said you couldn't spend the day with the dark haired one and I wasn't so keen on the other boy so we made a plan between us.'

'I suppose so. I'm feeling guilty now just remembering it.'

Leonie leaned forward and squeezed her sister's arm.

'But remember the night when Spikey Wilson missed his train home and he had to come back with us?'

'Oh, yes, and it was late and we smuggled him in to the house…!'

'And we were sitting having coffee in the lounge, whispering in case we woke mum and dad and then, suddenly, dad was standing there in his dressing gown… 'What's going on here?'

'He thought we were smuggling a boyfriend in!'

'And Spikey jumped up without warning and said, 'Laurence Wilson, Sir,' and shook dad's hand! We both looked at each other 'cos we never knew his name was really Laurence and calling dad Sir!' They laughed hysterically, the Blonde rolling back on the sofa until Leonie continued.

'Dad was quite impressed and said he could stay in the spare room but he gave us that look before he went back to bed, that look that said 'No High-jinks!''

They were silent for a moment, firmly entrenched in the past.

'I'm going to miss you. I'll miss you terribly…but I'll get used to it.'

Sitting late into the night, they made promises to have regular flights to see each other in the coming year before wearily climbing the stairs to bed well after midnight.

Sunday came. The Blonde was eager for Black to collect her. Goodbyes had been said and she was impatient to start their life together. After breakfast, there was an urgent ring on the doorbell. Leonie and the Blonde exchanged questioning glances as no one was expected so early. Leonie answered the door and the Blonde could hear muffled voices coming from the hall. When she looked up, Philip was standing in the doorway, thin and unkempt, a day's growth on his chin.

'Phillip! What are you doing here?' she asked irritably.

He stood motionless, like a tall, gaunt soldier then moved slowly towards her.

'I'm sorry…so sorry,' he whispered taking her hand.

She started to panic and drew back from him.

'What is it? What's happened?' she screamed.

'There's been an accident. It's Black,' he said solemnly.

'Black? Where is he? What happened? Is he OK?' she asked. He waited for a moment wondering how he could tell her.

'I'm afraid not,' he said slowly, 'He died in the crash.'

Hearing his words, the Blonde fell to the ground in a state of hysteria. Her whole life spun before her.

'Not Black! No! Not Black!' she wailed in disbelief. Her future had disappeared. 'He was my life. He can't have gone. He wouldn't do that to me. We were going to spend the rest of our lives together…' She sobbed and allowed Philip to cradle her in his arms while Leonie, tears spattering her face, stood at her side, stupefied.

'But how? When?' Leonie stammered.

'It was sometime last night,' Philip whispered, making it obvious that he did not want to say anything further in front of the Blonde. They tried to placate her, tried to make her lie down, gave her brandy for the shock but she was inconsolable.

'Where is he?' she shouted, 'I must see him? I've got to see Black!' and grabbing her coat, she made for the door. Leonie followed.

'You can't drive! You mustn't drive!' and pulled her back. Philip stepped forward and said sadly, 'I'll drive you.'

The Blonde stopped sobbing momentarily and their eyes met. He was genuinely distressed. At that moment she hated him for still being alive and launched herself at him, battering and hammering his chest with her fists, trying to release the agony inside her.

'You did it! You did this, you bastard! You took him away from me! You didn't want us to be together!'

Leonie pulled her away from Philip, who looked devastated, and enveloped her in her arms, soothing her as best she could and leading her to a chair. The Blonde, a crumpled mass, sat down and eventually murmured 'sorry' in Philip's direction. When she was more composed and ready, Phillip drove her to the hospital mortuary.

On the journey, they passed several newspaper billboards which Phillip could not hide from her. She learned the truth and her pain intensified even though she felt it could never get worse. The newspapers were full of it.

**'Black Lomax dies in fatal crash!'**
**'Tycoon's daughter in car with Lomax'**
**'Heiress fights for life!'**

Each new headline renewed her pain. The truth had finally revealed itself. Black had been with Andrea.

Her pale, drawn face looked down at his. She hardly recognised the empty shell which lay in repose. Gone were the carefree lines, the handsome tanned skin, those magnetic eyes. Instead, a hollow mask faced her. How old he looked. Death had left its agonising mark. She tried to visualise the handsome face which had shared her pillow for all those months but it was gone.

'So it happened,' she whispered, 'I thought it would. It was all a game to you!' and she started to cry. 'Death gave you away, revealed the man you really were. You couldn't resist her, could you?'

A shiver ran through her as she relived the moment they told her that Andrea had been found at his side. The deceit would always be with her like a pain that refused to go away. Her suspicions had been correct. Andrea had eaten into her life with one aim in mind.

She touched his icy cheek almost afraid to feel the cold marble which had once felt so warm as he lay next to her. She withdrew her hand quickly, the closeness of him had caught her breath.

'I loved you but perhaps that was a weakness in me.'

Unwilling to pull herself away, she bent down and kissed his forehead, desperately fighting with mixed emotions. A last glance and she abruptly turned and walked from the room, his last words to her left with the farm worker who found him.

Philip stood outside. She hesitated when she saw him. He looked older and yet almost like a small boy. His hair was a tangled mass and his eyes were bloodshot, ringed with black hollows, staring from a face with a grey pallor. He caught her hand as she passed him.

'Let me take you home,' he pleaded, his eyes appealing, hoping that she would say 'yes'.

'And Andrea…?' she questioned coldly.

'She means nothing to me. We're finished! It was always you!' he mumbled.

'And the baby…?'

'There was no baby! It was all a lie! She made it all up! Come home with me, please?' he begged.

She looked at him defiantly, practising her newly enforced independence.

'No, Phillip. There's no going back. The past has made us what we are. I'm sorry.'

Shrugging off his grip, she walked passed him into the courtyard, hands thrust deeply into the pockets of her raincoat. Her shadow darkened the paving stones, wet from the rain as Phillip stood hunched against the door, watching her fade into the mist, a slowly diminishing figure outlined against the dismal buildings, the click of her heels echoing on the paving stones and eating into his brain. For the first time in his life, he began to hate himself; his weakness, his foolishness, his rigidity, his everything. He slowly slid down the door frame and a crumpled body lay on the rain-soaked ground and cried. It was a fearful, lost cry which pierced the empty day.

Eduardo leaned against the side of the chauffeur-driven car, an expensive cigar clenched between his white teeth. His blonde, grey-flecked hair glistening from the descending mist as he pulled the collar of his overcoat closer round his neck to protect him from the cold. When he saw her he absentmindedly flung down the cigar and ran to meet her, enveloping her in his arms. She looked up at him with tears in her eyes.

'It's Ok, Kid! I'm here and I ain't going nowhere!'

'Oh, Ed, what would I do without you...but there's something I need to do.'

'You name it, Baby!'

He led her to the car with a protective arm round her shoulder and they drove off at speed.

The Blonde walked cautiously along the hospital corridor furtively looking in each private room. The atmosphere was heavy with a starched cleanliness and the overpowering smell of antiseptic. It reminded her of visiting Leonie after her suicide attempt. She felt suddenly dizzy and sat down on a chair in the corridor. As she tried to calm herself, raised voices could be heard coming from a room near her.

'What the Hell av you done now? Do you realise the newspapers are full of it? What possessed you to get involved with Black Lomax again—the same bastard I warned you against all those years ago?'

The man's voice rose higher as he became more agitated. She recognised it as that of Winston Elliot Winbech III, Andrea's father. They had never met but everyone knew who he was. The Blonde was listening intently. When Winbech stopped for breath, there was only the faintest of responses from his subject.

'Oh, Daddy, please...'

'Don't 'Daddy' me, gal. And you made me find the fucking guy a job! You fooled me! I didn't know he was the same guy or I never would 'av done!' He paused to catch his breath. 'All your life I've been baling you out of one scrape or another...and I'm Goddam sick of it!'

'But Daddy...'

'And the newspapers! I can't get outta my car but they're swarming around, pushing, shouting, swearing at me for a story. I've gotta hide half the time! You're ruining my reputation, gal, and it's gotta stop! I Won't be able to get you outta this one, that's for sure! You understand?'

'Yes, Daddy...' came the faint reply as the Blonde heard movements from within and approaching steps. Winbech III pushed brusquely through the door, grim faced, followed by a large man whom the Blonde thought would be a bodyguard.

She waited nervously as their footsteps disappeared down the corridor then she tentatively looked through the window and saw for the first time, Andrea Winbech lying on the bed. She lay amongst a mass of tubes, her whole body swathed in white bandages, pulleys supporting parts of her. A strand of thick red hair escaped from the head bandages and partially hid the stitches to her face. The Blonde felt no sympathy. Here was the woman who had destroyed her life. She could only feel hatred.

She walked slowly to the door and pushed it open. Andrea looked at her in astonishment.

'What the hell are you doing here?' she whispered frantically as the Blonde moved towards her. 'Nurse! Nurse!' She tried to shout but her strangled attempt died on the air. She struggled to find the little red emergency button but the Blonde sprang forward and snatched it away from her. The Blonde's mouth was dry.

'You know who I am, don't you? You've always known.'

Andrea looked steadily at her.

'Of course I know who you are! You tried to take Black from me but you didn't succeed!' A grotesque cackle rose from the depths of her throat and the Blonde stepped back. 'And you won't succeed now! He's mine forever! He was always mine! You should have known that!'

Anger burst inside the Blonde and she stepped forward. Her reaction was to pull the tubes from their housing to silence Andrea forever. It was very tempting but wasn't in her nature.

'You're not worth it!' she thought and bent close to Andrea's face. For the first time, she could see the fear in her enemy's eyes. It empowered her.

'Don't think you'll get away with this! I haven't finished with you yet!' and the Blonde knocked her plastered arm. Andrea squirmed and let out an injured scream. 'You've ruined my family…!' Andrea interrupted.

'You should be thanking me! I sent your husband back to you! OK. Jeff was a mistake. I got the wrong guy. But it's ok to fuck up sometime!'

'Fuck up! Is that how you see the devastation you've left behind?' She stood up. 'You are one crazy bitch! I almost feel sorry for you…but you're going to pay for what you've done!'

She quickly left the room, trying to forget the horror which connected them.

# Nineteen

Eduardo was waiting for her as she left the hospital and insisted that she stay with him temporarily at his Chelsea apartment.

'There's no way you're going back to that house. Phillip will be there! You don't need all that at this point in time. You need friends around you and Brett and I will see that you're well looked after!' The Blonde was too shattered to argue and grateful to be led away like a lost child who needed protection.

A few days later, the media was full of the news that Black's death might not have been an accident and that the police were questioning two eye witnesses who had come forward. The autopsy had found that Black was medically fit and had no alcohol or drugs in his system. A police spokesman said that the car was mechanically sound and that driving conditions were excellent. He also said that they would be interviewing the other passenger in the vehicle—Andrea Winbech—as soon as she was well enough to be questioned. Could Andrea have had anything to do with Black's death? The thought chilled the Blonde.

'I never guessed that you and Black were together!' Eduardo said one evening before dinner. The Blonde watched from the sofa as he sliced onions, the rhythmic chopping sound clattering above his conversation. 'I've known Black for quite a long time and he seemed so much happier lately. I thought it might be this Winbech dame that Brett saw him with at the Ritz... never realised it was you...' He hesitated for a moment. 'Oh, sorry...I shouldn't have said that...stuck my big foot in it.'

He turned from the work surface to the cooker and threw the onions into a huge pan where they sizzled and spat throwing a comforting odour into the air. The Blonde left her position on the sofa and took a stool at the middle island.

'It's OK. Don't worry about it. I've got to get used to the idea that Black was seeing her as well as me.' She thought about her relationship with Black and the long nights and days of subterfuge, always being on edge in case they were discovered and the media got hold of the story. 'I'm not surprised you didn't know about Black and I. We were very discreet, never going anywhere that he might be recognised and spending most of our time outside London in a very remote hotel...' then she remembered that was where he had been found and broke down crying.

'Hey, honey, I didn't mean to upset you by bringing up the subject,' Eduardo said, putting his arm round her and trying to calm her. 'You should have let me in on your secret and I could have helped you both!'

'Thanks, Ed, but it's too late now,' she sobbed then looked at him and a smile broke over her face. 'You've got something on your cheek. I think it's onion peel!' She wiped it away and they both laughed.

Eduardo fell silent and turned to his task. Juicy chicken breasts lay ready and he smeared them with oil before rubbing in herbs and seasoning. It was difficult to know what to say or do. She was grieving as he was too but in a much smaller way. He had liked Black a lot, thought him one of the good guys and their paths had crossed a lot in Britain and the USA not to mention starring in 'The Wasp' together. There would be a big hole left in his life but it would be worst for her. She had been about to start a new life in a new country with Black. What must she be feeling? All he could do was be there for her. And now the court case would be coming up soon and it would drag up all these emotions again. He tried not to let her see newspapers and tried to keep the television news off as much as possible but sometimes her mobile would alert her to the case and this would be followed by her despair.

'Oh no!' she shouted, 'I don't believe it!'

'What's happened?' he asked running to her side and looking over her shoulder. She read from her phone.

'Eye witnesses have told police about a mystery blonde who had been seen recently travelling in the area with Black Lomax!'

'Geez! You'll have to go to the police and clear this up or it won't go away,' Ed said, 'You've got nothing to hide. Everyone you care about knows already and the Police will just be wanting background information.'

She looked at him with watery eyes.

'You're right. Will you come with me? I don't like to ask, but I feel pretty shaky…'

'You don't need to ask, Baby! Of course I will!'

The Blonde and Ed spent a couple of hours at the Police Station. It was dark when they emerged but even then there was a newspaper reporter waiting with a cameraman. He thrust a microphone into her face.

'Are you the mystery blonde the police were searching for?'

She stayed tight-lipped but the camera kept flashing as Ed pushed them aside shouting.

'Hey, guys! Give us some space!' and rushed her to his car.

'Wasn't that Eduardo Costello?' the reporter asked his accomplice who looked blankly back,' I'm sure it was him!'

Hearing his name mentioned, Eduardo rushed her into the vehicle and asked Max, his driver, to hurry. They screeched off into the night before any more photographs could be taken. But it was too late. The evening press bore huge headlines which she could not ignore.

**'Mystery Blonde Unveiled!'**

Below was a grainy photo of Ed and the Blonde in the doorway of the Police Station, her blonde hair stark against the darkness. There followed a paragraph which revealed her name and that she had been having an affair with Black Lomax. It went on to say that Eduardo Costello was consoling the Blonde. She looked at it in horror but Ed shrugged his shoulders. He was used to the intrusion of his privacy.

'Don't let it worry you! These hacks say anything to sell their drivel. If they can't get a story, they invent one!' There was no reaction as she sat staring at the newspaper. 'Anyway, you don't mind being linked to me, do you? He teased.

She gave him a shy smile and read on.

After the events of that evening, the Blonde was in an emotional state. She flopped onto the sofa on their return from the Police Station and closed her eyes. She was distraught. Reliving the past months in her statement had exposed again the enormity of her situation, something she had been trying to contain for the last few days. The whole essence of her life had been eroded, worn thin like a piece of old fabric and only the threads were left exposing the spaces in between. Black had gone forever and Phillip was no longer part of her future. She felt so alone.

Ed's apartment was luxurious befitting his star quality but it wasn't a home. It was a temporary fix for him while in London. The place was a bachelor pad where everything was clean cut and utilitarian. She longed for familiarity and the comfort of having her possessions around her to give her some consolation.

'Hey, dreamer!' Ed said gently, handing her a glass of wine, 'You need this after the day you've had.' And he sat down beside her. She drank the ice cold liquid and felt its progress through her body. He could tell she was sinking deeper into despair and wanted to protect her from herself.

'Thanks, Ed. I need a drink. Some anaesthetic... help me to forget.'

'I know, Kitten, I know exactly how you feel,' and he put his arm around her and drew her towards him. When he used the word 'Kitten' she shuddered as it reminded her of Black and an ache rose to her throat. She rested her head on his shoulder and could smell the faint remnants of aftershave. She had missed this sort of intimacy. They sat this way for some time then Ed jumped up, refilled their glasses and put on some soft, soothing music.

'You like this sound?' he asked. She nodded in agreement and he pulled her up from the sofa. 'Hey, let's have a dance! It'll do you good.' She felt limp, like a rag doll, the wine having relaxed her but she allowed him to pull her up and enclose her in his strong arms. For the first time in weeks, she felt safe. They swayed to the music in the dimly lit room, the warmth of his body penetrating hers. She wanted to stay this way forever, feeling close to someone, feeling safe but Ed interrupted.

'Let's up the tempo!' he said and left her while he changed the music. For a moment, she felt lost and vulnerable but he returned and pulled her into his arms, gently manipulating her body over the floor to the manic beat which got faster and faster. Drawing apart, they laughed and shouted to each other above the music, gyrating across the floor in different directions and then bouncing back to each other or bumping into furniture in a wild, frenzied jig of abandonment.

When the music finished, they flopped onto the sofa, breathless, laughing. After a few minutes rest, Ed opened another bottle of wine and they drank it without noticing while they talked about their childhoods and families and America. She watched his animated face, strong, vivacious and she longed for him to hold her again. She felt mellow, the wine having temporarily washed away her terrors. She snuggled up to him and he looked at her curiously then drew her towards him and kissed her. It was a nice kiss and she responded but he drew back quickly.

'Hey, I'm sorry! I shouldn't have done that. I wasn't thinking…'

She pulled him back and said nothing but they kissed again, this time more passionately, more urgently as his hands caressed every inch of her body.

'Let's go to bed,' he whispered and he lifted her up and carried her to his bedroom where the Blonde lay naked in his arms. They were uninhibited as they discovered each other in the darkness, under the duvet. New body. New skin. A frantic coupling of two bodies began and endured until the early hours.

The morning broke gently into night, chipping away at her consciousness, noises making her aware of the wakening world. She turned in bed feeling the warm body next to hers. Her head was pounding like a thousand hammers were at work. She felt sick. His handsome face lay in repose, gently breathing. The events of last night came crashing back to her. He had been a considerate lover and there had been a little passion but it wasn't her passion. Her passion had died with Black. It was a need in that moment which satisfied. She sat on the edge of the bed, holding her sore head and wondering where to go.

'Come back to bed, Honey!' His voice startled her and she turned swiftly to look at him. His eyes were still closed and there was a faint smile on his lips. He could tell how she was feeling. 'I know, it should never have happened. That's what you're thinking.' His eyes were still closed.

'I feel bad,' she said, 'I feel I've been unfaithful to Black…that I'm a bad person!'

He stretched his suntanned arm over to her and took her hand gently in his. He suddenly opened his eyes. They were bright blue, penetrating the early morning light and startling her. There was no doubt he was devastatingly handsome and maybe she could forgive herself for having fallen for him a little while she was vulnerable.

'Don't beat yourself up, Baby! It was fun, wasn't it?' She lay back on the bed next to him. Her mouth was dry and she was desperate for a cold drink. 'Come on,' he said rolling her over towards him, 'Let's get outta here! We need fresh air and food! I'll take you for some breakfast. How's that sound?'

The thought of food made her want to throw up. Ed leapt out of bed without waiting for a reply and she watched his naked body move across the room. Eduardo Costello. The name had always meant something to her from the silver screen. She had never considered it before as he had always been just Ed to her, an ordinary guy and now, here she was, having spent the night with that ordinary guy. Together, they had stepped over the boundary of friendship.

Over breakfast, she hugged a mug of black coffee and watched Ed eat heartily. Last night seemed not to have affected him. The warm liquid was helping to clear her head a little. It felt strange sharing breakfast with him. She watched him cut into Eggs Over Easy and followed the ooze of the silky yellow yolk making its way over his plate.

'I've got to go home!' she said suddenly.

Ed crunched a mouthful of toast.

'Sure,' he said, 'I'll get Max to drive us there. You wanna pick up some clothes or something?'

His eyes were clear blue and every time he looked straight at her, she found them more and more appealing.

'No, I mean I've got to go back there to stay. This isn't going to work.'

'What's not gonna work?' he asked almost absent-mindedly.

'Me staying at your place.'

Ed put down his knife and fork and surveyed her. His mouth cracked into a smile.

'Look, Honey, last night was never meant to happen but it was a great night! We had fun, didn't we? You're not going 'cos of last night, are you?' She looked down at her hands clasping the coffee cup. 'Oh, Babe, don't take life so seriously. I like you…I like you a lot. Who knows. Given time this could develop but it's the wrong time for you. You can stay with me until after the court case…no strings…! When your head is clearer then we can take it from there. How does that sound?' He smiled, revealing his white, even teeth then he reached over and stroked her cheek. 'Come on! You must be feeling a bit better now. Let's see a smile.' She grinned. 'That's better!' He took a gulp of coffee and she noticed how square and strong his hands were. 'Besides, you can't go back home! Phillip's there!'

He was right. She didn't want to see Phillip far less stay in the same house as him. Ed was so calm. Nothing seemed to disturb his equilibrium. He was mature and sensible, took everything on board and dealt with it instantly. It made her feel safe. The longer she spent with him, the more comfortable she became but she did not want to admit this to herself.

Ed opened the newspaper which he had brought with him as it had been delivered that morning.

'Geez! Listen to this, Honey,' he said as he studied the story.

'What is it?'

'It's only about Andrea Winbech.' The Blonde froze. 'New evidence suggests she had something to do with it and she's been arrested! Wow! I can't believe it!' The Blonde could believe it and she shook inside thinking that Black could still be with her if it hadn't been for Andrea Winbech. He noticed that she had gone ashen white. 'Hey, don't think about it. We'll get through this together, you and me.'

'Don't come to the front of the house and come after dark! They're all there, buzzing about like flies!' Peggy said, 'They've been camped outside for days but they usually go about ten...better go round the back and I'll let you in,' she hesitated for a moment, 'You know the house is up for sale, don't you?' The Blonde was shocked. Phillip had never told her he intended doing this. 'He hasn't been here for weeks. I've been going in and keeping an eye on things but he might 'av said 'e wasn't staying here.'

She told Ed what was happening and they arranged to meet Peggy at the house. Ed dressed in his darkest jogging bottoms, dark top and a ski hat hiding his hair. He urged her to do the same. When they were both kitted out, they laughed at each other's appearance.

'We don't want to be seen! Especially if someone thinks we're burglars!' and they chuckled together like two naughty children having an adventure.

Peggy walked across the road in the darkness. The assembled journalists and photographers became alert as she approached and formed a circle round her. She pushed them out of the way as she moved onto the drive but they scrambled amongst themselves to get near her.

'Get outta me way!' she shouted and they backed off a little. 'You ain't gonna get a story tonight so you might as well do yourselves a favour and go home!'

They all started at once.

'Where's Rachel Mason?'

'Is it true Phillip Mason was having an affair with Andrea Winbech?'

'Was Black Lomax Rachel Mason's lover?'

It made her angry. As she set foot on the gravel driveway, she turned round sharply.

'Look! I'm saying nothing. You are just a loada leeches, burying into people's private lives and splashing it all over your papers. Well, you can clear off! I'm going into the house, which is empty, to check on things and, if you're still here when I get out, I'm phoning the police 'cos you're trespassing!'

They all looked down to see that they were standing on private ground and started to back away.

'Give us a story, Missus!' one shouted and he tripped backwards over a garden pot. 'What's your name? Can't you tell us anything?'

She turned away and stood on the doorstep.

'You've been warned!'

Opening the door, she disappeared inside.

Meanwhile, Max dropped Ed and the Blonde at the end of the lane which ran at the back of the house. Ed got to the gate which was locked and heaved himself up effortlessly onto the wall.

'You wait here until I open the gate for you,' and she could hear him drop onto the ground on the other side. 'Shit!' he said under his breath.

'What is it?' she asked anxiously.

'It's OK. Just ripped my joggers on a sharp edge on top of the wall.'

'Are you OK?'

'Sure, I'll live.' And she could hear him opening the lock on the gate. He smuggled her in and clasped her in his arms for a moment. She could feel the cold night air on his face as their cheeks met.

'My accomplice!' he laughed then they heard the back door creak open and Peggy standing there beckoning them to come quietly.

'They are still outside on the pavement,' she whispered as she hugged the Blonde.

She looked wide-eyed at Ed whose frame seemed to dominate the small lobby. He put out his hand and smiled.

'Hi, Peggy, I'm Ed. Thank you for helping us get in.'

She was almost speechless but clasped his hand, her eyes sparkling with recognition.

'I know who you are and I'm so glad to meet you,' she said coyly, 'I've seen most of your films…and I can't believe you're here.'

'Just most…' He laughed, 'Not all?' She blushed and he hugged her. 'I'm only teasing you, Peggy. I'm very glad to be here and to meet you!'

Peggy said she would put the kettle on as she had made sure there was tea and coffee when she came over in the week. The Blonde ran upstairs and started to pack a case with all the bits and pieces she held dear plus a few more winter clothes. There were masses of things she wanted to take but they would have to be left until later.

Downstairs, Ed was looking at the rip in his trousers while Peggy poured coffees. Blood oozed from the tear and the Blonde was concerned.

'Let me look at it.' She insisted.

'It's nothing,' he said, pulling back the fabric, 'Just a scratch!'

Peggy set the coffees down.

'It might just be a scratch but you need something on that. Best be on the safe side.'

She went into the kitchen and they could hear her rummaging in drawers and reappearing with warm water, cotton wool and some antiseptic cream.

'Wow,' sighed Ed, 'I'm getting the full treatment!' as the Blonde and Peggy cleaned up the wound. When they had cleared away, they talked about the house sale.

'One day, they came and just put up the sign,' Peggy said, 'I was shocked. I knew you would have told me if you 'ad known but 'e never said nothing to me…nevers even came over to say he was going so I 'aven't seen hide nor hair of him for the last few weeks…don't know where he's gone.'

The Blonde wondered if he had gone to stay with his brother in South London but she didn't care where he had gone. She was angry that he hadn't told her about his intentions and that she had to find out this way.

'Don't you worry, lovey, I'll look after the place until it's sold.' She turned to Ed. 'You'll look after her for the time being, I'm sure you will.' And she smiled sweetly at him.

'Of course I will.'

She accompanied them into the back garden, lit only by the yellow glare of the street lights. Opening the back gate, they kissed each other quietly and said goodbyes in whispers. AS the gate closed behind Peggy, Ed grabbed the case.

'Come on. Cinderella, let's go!'

She laughed and they sprinted off along the lane to where Max was parked.

# Twenty

She woke sharply and remembered it was that day, the day she had been dreading for weeks, the day of the court case. Her room was dark and sunless which seemed apt for the way she was feeling and a heavy mist lay on the landscape like thick, grey flannel. Memories hit her like crazy thunderbolts crashing into her brain. She tried to crush them as though mentally stamping on them but they kept recurring. They were all blurred like looking through a rain-soaked window. Sketches of Black by the lake or images of them together in bed kept slithered into her mind like unwanted souvenirs. The Blonde suddenly felt very alone.

Since the night that she and Ed had fallen into bed together, she had stayed in one of his spare rooms and this had worked well until now. Something was driving her forward and she seemed powerless to halt it. She crept through to Ed's bedroom which was washed in a pale blue radiance and could hear him breathing softly as he slept. Everything was quiet. Tip-toeing to the edge of his bed, she watched him sleeping. He looked so peaceful. She stood there for a few moments devouring his handsome face. Her eyes lingered on his thick blonde hair flecked with grey and imagined her fingers threading their way through it. She wanted to kiss his firm lips and feel his flesh next to hers. The urge was so great that she gently pulled back the duvet and slid in beside him like a thief in the night. She needed him now more than ever. He turned without opening his eyes and smiled, putting his arm round her and drawing her closer to him so that she could feel the warmth of his skin against hers. She kissed his firm lips following their outline with her tongue until there came a response. She could feel his hardness against her thigh and knew that he wanted her as much as she wanted him. Soon he was inside her and they moved together in an abandonment of ecstasy and elation. Later, they lay silently in each other's arms. Unlike Black, she and Ed had spent time doing ordinary things together and getting to know each other. Now she felt complete and knew the time was right for them to be together.

Max dropped Brett, Ed and the Blonde at the court entrance. The pavement was littered with journalists, photographers and cameramen. Brett pushed a pathway between them. As soon as they saw Ed, they rushed towards him, snapping like crocodiles and shouting his name.

'Mr Costello!'

'What do you think of Andrea Winbech, Ed?'

'Is she guilty?'

'Any comment?'

She froze at the onslaught but Ed put a protective arm round her and guided her through the crowd saying, 'Thank you, Gentlemen. No comment at the moment,' and smiled broadly. They rushed up the steps and into the quiet dignity of the courthouse. The Blonde was dreading hearing about the night Black died but knew she had to face it and get some closure.

The area outside the individual courtrooms was marble paved with great columns supporting the ceiling. Footsteps ate into the sobriety and quietly muttered conversations added a dismal despondency to the atmosphere. Even the faded blue light filtering in from the central dome on the ceiling seemed to throw gloom over the scene.

There were a few dark figures standing around in huddled groups, as though lost, but one stood alone.

'There's Black's Mom!' Ed pulled the Blonde towards her. 'Esther!' he cried as he approached the slight figure dressed in black. 'It's so good to see you.' And he hugged her tightly for a moment before he turned to the Blonde. 'Let me introduce you. Esther Lomax, this is Rachael Mason.'

The two women looked at each other for a moment. Esther's face oozed despair. Round peach-like cheeks dominated a pale face topped with Black's eyes. His mum was small and round like a little apple pie. She was wholesome and the Blonde could almost smell the scent of Corn Bread straight from the oven. But Black's eyes were full like a dam about to burst. Esther extended her gloved hand.

'Nice to meet you! Buddy told me so much about you during our long telephone conversations.' Buddy? Then she remembered it was the name his family gave him. 'He was so excited about you coming to the States.' She looked down at their clasped hands. 'We were all so proud of what he achieved.'

The Blonde stepped forward and the two women hugged for a long moment in mutual grief. This was not the way she had imagined meeting Black's mother and their pain became raw again.

The courtroom was packed for the high-profile case and a low muttering reigned as people shifted uneasily on their seats while they waited. The morning sun was high now and splinters of it slanted through the high wind0ows and fell on Andrea Winbech as she sat with her Defence team at the front. The Blonde swallowed hard when she saw her and tried to quell the hatred rising inside.

Brett, Ed and she sat at the very back for privacy. There were so many journalists ready to jump on any movement or expression either of them made which might then be fabricated into a story. Ed held her hand and was very attentive. She noticed a new intimacy in his glance.

When everyone was settled and the soft whisperings gradually stopped, a feeling of expectancy spread over the room as the Judge's hammer called for 'silence' then he introduced the case. His voice was clear, formal and chillingly echoed round the court. Then Gareth Hughes, for the Prosecution, made his opening statement. He was tall and commanding, his voice was rich and eloquent and reverberated around the vast hall. He dominated the space as he spoke mesmerising the listeners.

'Black Lomax was a very successful Hollywood actor having recently tasted the highest accolades in his profession. He was 'going places' as they say. He was young. He was handsome. He had his whole life before him,' Hughes stopped momentarily and surveyed the court. 'He was healthy. No problems there. There were no drugs or alcohol found in his bloodstream. No problems there. The car he was driving was mechanically sound and the driving conditions were excellent so no problems there either. So why did he die on that fateful night of October, 7th, 2019? There can only be one answer.

His companion on that night was Andrea Winbech, a woman who is used to getting what she wants, a woman who has spent the last year destroying the family of Black's companion with devastating consequences. This is a woman who has manipulated people, including her own father, to achieve her aims. In this case, her aim was to eliminate all competition for Black Lomax's affection.

When that was unsuccessful, she decided to destroy Black Lomax himself and I shall prove to you that this is exactly what she did.'

He sat down amidst unrest around the court as people absorbed the information. A few moments later the Judge asked Hughes to start the proceedings. The Prosecution then called their first eye witness, William Lamb, a farmer. The Blonde did not recognise him as being one of the workers in the field that she had passed so many times. Her mind had been focussed on Black.

Gareth Hughes stood tall and looked imperious as he held onto the lapels of his gown'

'Mr Lamb, is it correct that you have lived and farmed in the area where the accident occurred, and have done so, since you were a boy and that you know these surroundings very well?'

William drew himself up to his full height which was just average but his muscular build made him seem taller. His ill-fitting suit barely closed over his chest. It was a faded brown check and almost threadbare but there wasn't much need for a suit in William's life except for weddings and funerals. His hair was neatly brushed back from his face and thick with Brylcreem but some strands refused to sit down and stood determinedly upwards.

'That's correct, Sir,' he replied and the lawyer continued.

'Can you recall the events on the night of 7$^{th}$ October, this year?'

'Yes, Sir, I certainly can.' His voice was strong and his accent West Country. He stood straight like a soldier, his crumpled shirt and tie looking incongruous amongst the smart gowns of the law. He held tightly onto his bonnet as he spoke. 'My brother, Thomas, and meself were walking back to the farmhouse abouts three in the afternoon when we 'eard this car engine in the distance. As it got nearer we recognised the car as one that came these parts every few weeks or so. Nothing much ever 'appens in these parts…it very quiet so the big flashy car and 'im inside, stood out a mile, if you knows wot I means.'

'When you say 'him inside', to whom are you referring?'

William twisted the bonnet in between his hands. He was nervous. This was becoming an ordeal for him as he was not used to speaking in public. There were so many people staring at him.

'The man wot died in the crash! I didn't know his name then but now knows it to be Black Lomax.'

'So you saw the man you now know to be Black Lomax in the car on that evening. Was he alone in the car?'

'No, Sir, there was…that woman.' And he nodded in the direction of Andrea Winbech who sat with a vacant look on her face, staring into the distance.

'Do you mean Andrea Winbech?

'Yes, that's definitely the one he was with that night. He always 'ad the blonde one wiff him. That's why we were so surprised to see someone different that night.'

'When you say the 'blonde one', can you tell the court to whom you are referring?'

'The one in the papers. The mystery blonde! Rachel something. She's the one he was always with!'

The Blonde hung her head, her face reddening aware that all heads had turned in her direction. She played nervously with the fingers of her leather gloves. Ed stretched across and squeezed her hand but she didn't look up.

'The car must have been travelling at what…thirty or forty miles an hour as it passed you?'

'I would probably say about thirty if that, as there are lodsa bends around there and 'e was takin' it easy, I would say.'

'Did you get a good look inside the car as it passed, long enough to ascertain for certain that it was Andrea Winbech?'

'We did, me brother and meself 'cos the driver's window was open as it passed and we could hear her screamin' at him!'

'Screaming at Black Lomax?'

'Aye, and me brother, Thomas, commented on it at the time. He said she 'ad the eyes of the Devil and I told him not to be so daft but I did wonder as she was right up close, yellin' in Mr Lomax's face while he looked straight ahead.' There were audible muttering around the court and the judge called for silence. Andrea Winbech slouched forward on the table in front of her, held her chin on her hands and stared at William Lamb as if to threaten him. William noticed the movement and looked sideways at her. He looked edgy but continued bravely.

'What happened next?'

'Thomas and me was walking along after the car passed us, wondering 'oo she was and where the blonde one was, when we heard this almighty bang and crashing noise. Well, we took off in the direction it came from and a few minutes later, found the crash.' William leaned on the wooden edge of the witness box as he remembered the sight. 'It all happened so quickly.'

The lawyer for the prosecution paused while he looked down at his papers, pushed his spectacles further up his nose then continued.

'So in a matter of minutes, the car having gone passed you and your brother with the passenger allegedly screaming at the driver, had crashed into a tree?'

'Yes, sir, Half Way Tree as it is known in these parts.'

By this time, William was visibly shaking and the Judge asked if he would like to sit while he gave evidence. He nodded and a chair was brought into the witness box. Once seated, he drank from the water glass available, his large, work worn hands engulfing it. After a few moments, the Judge turned to the Prosecution lawyer and said, 'You may continue, Mr Hughes.'

'Thank you, Your Honour.' He paused for a moment then said, 'Mr Lamb, when you and your brother arrived at Half Way Tree minutes later, can you describe what you found there.'

'The car was well crushed. Thomas managed to get to the passenger and look for a pulse but he couldn't find one. We thought she was dead. We could see that the driver was caught under the steering wheel. He was still breathing but the door wouldn't open. We eventually crawled through a back door which we managed to force open and I could feel a pulse. I kept speakin' to him while Thomas tried to get a signal on his mobile phone to get the Emergency Services there.'

'You now know that the driver on that fateful night was Black Lomax?'

'Yes, Sir.'

'Did he speak to you?'

'He was very weak but I was close up to him and he was trying to speak. I could make out what he was saying. He said, 'Tell her it isn't true…tell her I love her…I didn't want this.' I said I would make sure I told her and then his pulse just weakened then faded altogether.'

The Blonde wiped tears from her eyes and clung to Brett's arm. She was trying to be strong but it was harrowing hearing all that had happened. When she heard Black's words, she understood what he was trying to tell her.

'To whom do you think Black Lomax was referring when he spoke those words?'

'The blonde one…cos the other one was wiff him and it didn't look like he'd be wanting to say them to her, not after she looked so threatening and screaming and everything.'

'Thank you, Mr Lamb. No more questions, Your Honour.'

William Lamb's ordeal was not yet over as Richard Royston for the Defence came before him and stood for a moment deliberating. He was a short, rotund man with a ruddy complexion from too much alcohol consumption. His voice was loud and harsh and demanded that he was noticed. William looked anxiously towards him.

'Mr Lamb, how good is your eyesight?'

William looked puzzled for a moment.

'Fairly good, I would says.'

'Just fairly good? Not perfect?' Royston asked. William looked at him blankly. 'The reason I'm asking is that you seem positive that Black Lomax's companion on the evening in question was Andrea Winbech. Considering your eyesight is only 'fairly good', is it possible that you could have been mistaken?'

William seemed flustered. He had been in the witness box for a long time and desperately wanted to be released but his resolve did not falter.

'Definitely not, Sir! It was she and nobody else.'

Royston held his chin in his hand and drew his fingers along its length as though searching for an imaginary beard. He referred to his papers and looked up to William.

'You say you heard screaming allegedly coming from Andrea Winbech as she passed you in the car. You have already claimed that the car was going at an approximate speed of thirty miles per hour. Black Lomax was driving so he would be closer to you as the car passed. I put it to you that your view of the passenger, Andrea Winbech, was obscured by the driver and that you did not hear any screaming. What you could have heard was laughter.'

William's attitude changed. He clenched his fists with anger.

'That's not true! She was nearly sittin' on his knee, she was that close to 'im—almost at a ninety degree angle to 'im! And she definitely wasn't laughing, not with that look on 'er face.'

Royston thanked the witness and returned to the Defence table. The Judge said that William could stand down and relief covered his face. Then his brother, Thomas, testified. He was cross examined and verified everything that William had said.

The day stretched on with statements being read, witnesses called and forensic evidence being examined. The partial palm print on the steering wheel seemed to be damning for Andrea.

Then it was over for the day. It had been exhausting. Everyone filed out of court like broken pieces of china swept into a pile. When the crush dispersed, Esther stood alone, staring into nowhere, a solitary figure in the vastness of the building. Ed caught up with her and invited her to dine with them. She looked at him, mystified and mumbled.

'His Paw couldn't come, you know. Said he couldn't face it.' Ed put a comforting arm around her shoulder. 'He loved Buddy so much. He was his pride and joy.'

Her face crumpled and she pulled out a crushed handkerchief to hide her pain.

Max drove the four of them through the London rush hour. The light was fading now and a blue grey hue lay over everything. Only the shop lights and the traffic lights brightened up the journey as they darted from one lane of traffic to another to make progress. Eventually, they reached the Savoy and Max dropped them at the doorway where they were ushered inside.

Over dinner, Brett tried to make light conversation but no one felt like eating far less talking. Each sat quietly with their own thoughts until Esther spoke. Her voice was sweet and mellow and melted into the silence like a spoon spreading honey. She turned to the Blonde.

'You will come visit, won't you?' Esther moved uneasily on her chair and checked the buttons on her coat. 'I have some things of Buddy's I want you to have.'

The Blonde opened her mouth to speak but then realised that she might never go to the States now that Black was gone. Ed noticed her consternation and interjected.

'Of course she will, Esther.' He caught Rachel's eye and she nodded in agreement, 'We both will.'

Esther seemed content with his answer and smiled sweetly at both of them.

# Twenty-One

The next day, Andrea Winbech was to be examined. Her father's money could not keep her out of court and all heads turned as she was called into the dock. Not yet fully recovered, she walked with a stick and the scars on her face were still visible on the once perfect olive skin. Despite this, she held her head up high and tossed back the thick mane of hair which rolled over her shoulders like a waterfall and swept down her back in multiple waves. It shone in the midday light which fell over the courtroom turning it first to gold then amber and, as she moved, into a deep burnt red. This was all accentuated by the cream suit she wore knowing the effect it would create. All eyes were on her. The Blonde tried not to look in her direction but her eyes were drawn to her and she had to admit that Andrea was still beautiful.

The slight figure stood defiantly in the dock being questioned about the fateful night while the Blonde sat grim faced at the back of the court, waiting anxiously for her responses. Gavin Hughes drew himself up to his full height and looked steadily at her.

'Andrea Winbech, can you tell the court when you first met Black Lomax?' She looked at him and smiled broadly exposing her even, white teeth.

'About eight years ago in Florida.'

Her voice was clear and rich with a slight American drawl and it seemed to resonate round the courtroom. Hughes ignored her attempts to captivate him with her eyes and she sensed this from his demeanour which made her slightly irritated.

'How old were you when you met Black Lomax?'

'Sixteen!' she barked at him, shrugging her shoulders. He ignored the gesture and continued turning to address the room as he put the next question.

'Sixteen. An enviable age but also an impressionable age. I believe you and Black Lomax, who was not much older, started an affair while you were staying at a hotel in Florida with your parents. Is that correct?'

'Yes,' she whispered, remembering that summer which had changed her life. She remembered the joy and also the pain.

'And is it not also true that your father forbade you from seeing Black Lomax?'

'True.'

'But you still saw him secretly which resulted in your pregnancy, a pregnancy that your parents made you terminate. Is that correct?'

She searched frantically in her suit pocket and pulled out a handkerchief to catch the tears which came cascading down her cheeks.

'That's correct,' she sniffed.

Gareth Hughes ignored her tears and his voice rose louder.

'At the end of the holiday, did you keep in contact with Black Lomax?'

'Yes, I wrote every day to him and he wrote to me.'

'You did indeed write every day to him,' he paused and looked at the jury, 'but he did not write to you every day, did he? He wrote one letter and then nothing. Then you found out that you were pregnant but you did not tell him. You waited until you could have your full revenge on Black Lomax, someone whom you felt had let you down, someone whom you thought, had abandoned you and left you to deal with the pain of it all.'

Andrea turned white. Her eyes were cold and dark.

'It's not true. We loved each other all those years.' She shifted unsteadily in the witness box as though she might faint. 'Can I sit?' she mumbled to the Judge who nodded in agreement and she sat and sipped from a glass of water. Gareth Hughes waited impatiently while she composed herself. He was becoming increasingly irritated by her behaviour.

'Can you tell the court why you and Black Lomax were travelling in this particular area on the night of October $7^{th}$?'

Andrea, fully recovered in a matter of minutes, smiled and looked straight at him. Her manicured fingers played with a strand of hair and her pink painted lips parted momentarily as though she was about to speak. She knew everyone was looking at her and she was enjoying it. Gareth Hughes shuffled from one foot to the other as he waited. Eventually, a childlike voice emanated from Andrea.

'Black and I were going away for the weekend. We were very much in love and wanted to finalise some plans before we flew to the States the following week!'

She spread her story of lies interspersed with sighs of regret and fake tears. The Blonde cringed. Hughes never looked up.

'Could your plans not have been finalised in London?

'No!' she said positively, 'We had to get away. He was pretty famous and we needed anonymity so he chose a place where he wouldn't be recognised.' She suddenly saw the Blonde in the gallery. 'Plus he was being pestered by a woman… a horrible woman…she was following him everywhere…he couldn't shake her off…!' Her voice started to rise uncontrollably as she stared at the Blonde. 'She was stalking him, following him everywhere and he couldn't stand it! She even threatened me when I was in hospital!'

The Blonde was seized by anger and moved forward in her seat. Ed tried to hold her back but it was too late and she sprang to her feet.

'She's lying!' she shouted. 'It's all lies!'

Chaos erupted around her as a hundred faces turned in her direction. People talked, and the noise grew louder until the Judge called for 'Silence' and warned Rachel that she would be removed if there were further outbursts. Ed pulled her down to her seat and put his arm round her.

'Everybody knows she's lying,' he whispered, 'You know that as much as I do. She's a jerk!'

Andrea smirked at the Blonde's reaction but Gareth Hughes ignored her response.

'Isn't it a fact that you knew Black Lomax was about to return to the States with Rachel Mason—'

'No! That's not true! He loved me!' she interrupted.

'—and that you did everything you could to prevent this happening?'

Her cheeks started to redden with anger. She began to tap on the edge of the dock with her fingers and was visibly shaking.

'No! I tell you! We were going away together!'

'On the night in question I believe you left Phillip Mason at your apartment in Cambridge Mansions. You had been having an affair with him for the last month? Is that correct?'

Her green eyes flashed and she lowered her head as she looked at him.

'Maybe,' she muttered and a buzz went round the court. Journalists scribbled furiously, heads bent over notebooks.

'Please answer the question!' the Judge boomed.

'Yes! OK! I was having a bit of fun!' she shouted irritably. 'Why not? Every girl has to have a bit of fun!' and she pouted her lips Monroe-style and stood back, an arrogant smile on her face. Hughes continued.

'Not only did you start an affair with Phillip Mason but previously, you had an affair with his brother-in-law, Jeff!'

'He was a mistake!' She shouted angrily banging her fist on the edge of the witness box.

'A mistake? You destroyed his family, ruined his life and you call it a 'mistake'! I put it to you that you were so obsessed with Black Lomax that you would go to any lengths to separate him from Rachel Mason. If you couldn't have him, no one else would!' Hughes voice rose higher and louder. 'We have it on good authority that he was in love with Rachel Mason and they planned to go to the States and get married. You couldn't let this happen, could you, so you plotted, planned and devastated her whole family in an attempt to get your own way. When this didn't work, you calculatingly fabricated a story to get Black on his own and you deliberately and callously pulled the steering wheel from him to make the car crash. Is that not the case?'

Hughes took a deep breath after delivering his monologue. The court was silent but journalists still scribbled.

'No.' she whispered, almost inaudibly.

Hughes examined his papers then turned to the Judge.

'No more questions, Your Honour.'

Some individuals shifted on their seats adding an audible creaking to the mutterings of relief which passed round the court. It had been a long, gruelling session for everyone.

The burly figure of Richard Royston for Andrea's Defence, rose from his chair with some commotion, clearing his throat as he did so, being the type who demanded attention. He cut a pompous figure as he marched to the front ready to question Andrea and listen to her uttering vicious lie after lie while he pontificated on her innocence. It was an onerous prospect for the Blonde. She turned to Ed.

'I can't take any more of this,' she sighed. Her sweet, warm breath brushed his cheek and he sympathised.

'Whadda you say we get outta here?' he smiled and clasped her hand tightly as they quietly left through the back entrance where there were no journalists or photographers waiting for them.

Out in the fresh air, they relaxed and laughed nervously with pent up emotion. They hugged each other and pulled their winter coats tighter round their bodies as the wind whipped up dried leaves around their ankles. The sky was a dark, metallic grey.

'Looks like it might snow,' the Blonde said wearily.

'Lemme get you home!' Ed pulled her protectively towards him and they walked to where Max was waiting for them.

After dinner, it snowed. Lightly at first then great big cotton wool balls fell silently from the sky, stealthily wrapping the view in white. Sitting in Ed's lounge, they curled up on the sofa with just the light of a few candles glowing in the dark. From the window, they could see right over London and watch the shimmering city lights pulsating through the snowfall. The scene was mesmeric and it made Rachel think of Christmases past and family times. Her thoughts turned to Black.

'It seems so unfair that something which happened when he was very young should follow him all these years later and then cause his death…'

Ed pulled her closer.

'Yeah, he was one unlucky guy to get mixed up with that woman. She is one mad broad but she won't get away with it, don't worry.' He could see from the Blonde's watery eyes that the process was having an adverse effect on her. 'Hey, let's not bother going back for the rest of the case. We can get the verdict from the news…and Brett will fill us in! She's going down anyway! Whadda ya say?'

Rachel turned to him.

'Do you really mean that? You don't mind missing it?

He shook his head so she threw her arms round him, hugging her hard. After a few minutes he held her at arms' length and said,

'Why don't we get outta this place altogether?' She looked surprised. 'Well, you were going to the States anyway. Why don't you come with me! It'll do you good to get out of the country for a while, have a rest and we can see how things go from there. Whadda you say?'

Rachel looked out at the falling snow. It had changed the landscape from grey to a dazzling white.

'I'd like that very much,' she said.

Andrea moved nervously along the windowless corridor of her new world. Every little noise grew huge and echoed around her, accentuating her isolation and loneliness.

In an instant, she became aware of them. They stood in a foursome stretching along the wall, expressions morose. Standing in various positions, they looked mean. One was slouched against the cold tiles, playing with her braided hair, her neighbour chewed gum while a third girl stared vacantly into the distance. Signs of their past lives marked them; a broken nose, a facial scar, dark circles under eyes. The fourth was more alert. She was taller than the others with dark, oily hair which hung in strands to her shoulders. She had small beady eyes like black marbles and looked evil. As Andrea attempted to walk passed she jumped forward to bar her way.

'Oh look! It's the little Missy Heiress, all the way from Amerikay!'

The others seemed to wake up and they all slithered towards her like snakes in a sack. They crowded round, smirking and attempting to touch her red hair. Andrea froze.

'Fuck off!' she hissed nervously.

'Oh, touchy, touchy!' sneered the ring leader, her dark eyes narrowing as she eyed Andrea. 'Killed any nice actors lately?'

They all sniggered. She tried to ignore them and made to walk on but they crowded more closely forming a circle round her. The leader came closer, mimicking a child's voice.

'Oh Daddy! Daddy! They're being horrid to me! Help me Daddy!' as she put her arms over her chest in mock fear. The others screamed with laughter. Andrea was angry now. She turned quickly to her and spat the words, 'Screw you!'

But the ringleader was unconcerned and jumped back pretending to be surprised.

'I thought you were the one doing all the screwing!' she wisecracked.

This made the group worse and the laughter rose. Andrea pushed forward making her way along the corridor but they were fast on their feet and before she realised, she was pinned against the wall with the ringleader breathing into her face. Andrea could smell the bitterness of stale tobacco. Her eyes held a curious expression, somewhere between mischief and evil intent. Andrea turned away but the ringleader grabbed her hair and swung her back.

'Go, Rosella. Go, Rosella,' the others chanted menacingly under their breath as she stretched her arm over Andrea's shoulder so that there was no escape. She was so close that Andrea could smell the dankness of her clothes and see the malice in her eyes.

'Listen, little girl! You ain't in Daddy's house no more so you better get used to it, no shit!'

Andrea started to sweat. She had never had dealings with people like these. To her, they were a different species. Suddenly, a large shadow loomed over them.

'Break it up!' a warden shouted and the group dispersed in seconds. Andrea was shaken and cowered against the wall. 'Get to your cell, Winbech!'

'You gotta get me outta this fuckin' place! It's not safe! There are some crazy bitches in here! I'm shit scared! Do you understand me? Shit scared! Get my dad to…'

She screamed obscenities at her solicitor until he managed to quieten her.

'Sit down, Andrea, and calm down!' He spoke sternly. 'Shouting at me is not going to do any good. You must remain calm.' She knew he was serious and sat on the chair he indicated. 'Your father has done as much as he can. He has assured me that he can do no more. You'll be fortunate to get away with Manslaughter …'

'Holy shit!' she interrupted, the realisation hitting her. She covered her face with her hands hoping that it would all go away.

'Obviously, after the verdict, we can appeal for a transfer of prison so that you get put in a nicer place. This is just a temporary measure. There are other places…'

Andrea wasn't listening. She was fingering the tiny, sharp stone in her pocket. She had found it that morning in the exercise yard.

# Twenty-Two

'No! No! Don't shoot! Put the gun down!' Ed screamed, outstretched hand shaking, he fell to his knees in a crumpled mass, 'Please don't do this, Tommy, please don't!' he pleaded.

Rachel looked proudly on and smiled as Ed regained his composure and sat beside her on the sofa.

'Whadaya think?' he asked.

'I think you don't need me to tell you how to act,' she smiled.

'But do you think it's me? Do you think I'd be good in the part?' he asked eagerly, needing her approval.

'I think you'd be perfect!' she replied pulling him towards her and kissing his cheek.

Since they had abandoned the court case, Ed and Rachel had spent the days quietly mostly in the apartment, sometimes driving to the coast for some lunch with Leonie, occasionally visiting Peggy or a quiet dinner just the two of them. Most of the time they read through scripts and Rachel helped Ed, sometimes taking a part herself to make it seem more real for him.

One day, while Rachel and Ed were planning their future in America, Brett came to the flat. He was visibly excited and had several newspapers under his arm.

'Guilty!' he shouted, waving a newspaper above his head. Rachel and Ed looked at each other. They had tried to block out the court case and had never returned. Their daily routine had omitted any reference to Andrea Winbech and Black's death but Brett had brought it all crashing back. 'It's all over! They found her guilty! She's got ten years!'

He sat down with a flourish on the settee and they joined him on either side as he gleefully read from the newspaper.

*Heiress, Andrea Winbech, was today found guilty of causing the death of her former lover, Black Lomax.*

The word 'lover' made Rachel wince and she remembered the feelings she had had for Black. Then she remembered that he had betrayed her. Brett's voice bored into her brain.

*The accused wept into a handkerchief as the verdict was pronounced. Winbech is accused of Manslaughter and has been given a sentence of ten years...blah, blah, blah...* Brett paused momentarily to look first at Rachel then at Ed. 'This is massive! She's got what she deserved. Daddy even refused to get her bail!' He smiled victoriously then leafed through the newspaper until he found parts he thought they should hear.

'Well, thank the Lord for that!' Ed said, stretching his legs out in front and giving Brett more arm space. Rachel smiled but said nothing. It all seemed part of someone else's life now and didn't belong to her any longer.

'Hey, listen to this! Royston gives his closing statement. *Andrea Winbech is a victim, not a perpetrator. Andrea Winbech is not responsible for the death of Black Lomax—she loved him! Why would she want to kill him? She had loved him since they first met in Florida aged sixteen. Both were young but they had a relationship which resulted in her pregnancy.'*

The Blonde looked horrified and she exchanged glances with Ed while Brett continued.

'*She was forced to have an abortion by her parents and forbidden to see Black Lomax. This did not deter this poor, unfortunate woman from searching out Black Lomax and rekindling their affection for each other.* Huh!' muttered Brett almost to himself. 'Is this guy for real?' He turned the page of the broadsheet and balanced it on his knees so that Ed and Rachel could read along with him. '*She lost her baby and now she has lost her lover. She has been victimised in the press and media but you will find Andrea Winbech is innocent of causing the death of Black Lomax. Her only crime, if it be that, is that she loved him too much.* What a load of old bull! Can you believe he came out with all that garbage?'

Rachel looked at him.

'Nothing surprises me these days,' she said quietly, 'after all that's happened.'

'No, of course not. This must still be pretty raw for you. I'm sorry. I shouldn't be reading this out!' He patted her arm consolingly.

'No! You must. We need to know. You're right.' She turned in towards him and his newspaper. 'What did Gareth Hughes say in his summing up.?'

Ed jumped up.

'Keep talking. I'm listening but I'll fix us a drink.'

Brett turned back the pages.

'Gareth Hughes. Gareth Hughes.' He muttered under his breath as he looked through the story. 'Here it is! *Prosecution Barrister, Gareth Hughes, summed up by saying that Andrea Winbech had wilfully grabbed the steering wheel from Black Lomax and manipulated it in such a way as to cause the car to crash resulting in the death of Black Lomax. Hughes said that her plan to regain his affections had not succeeded and rage had consumed her. She was used to getting anything she wanted in life and could not take the rejection. The Barrister continued to state that the jury must take into account the forensic findings when making their decision. He was referring specifically to the finger prints and partial palm print found on the steering wheel showing that Andrea Winbech had held the wheel even though Black Lomax was driving. He finished with urging the jury to find her guilty as she wilfully caused his death.*'

Brett suddenly folded the newspapers together and laid them aside as Ed handed him a drink.

'Well,' Brett said, looking at Rachel, 'I guess that's enough of that! At least we know she won't be out for a very long time and you guys can get on with the rest of your lives!' He swallowed the drink in one as Rachel and Ed smiled at each other, 'I see you've started packing!' And nodded towards a neatly stacked pile of small boxes.

Rachel laughed.

'Oh yes, just a few things that mean a lot to me and I can't leave behind.'

'Any idea when you'll fly to the States?' Brett asked, looking in Ed's direction.

'Well, now that this is all over, we can go next week. Everything's in order ready to go. Rachel's been down to see Leonie and tied up loose ends.'

Rachel thought about Phillip, one of her loose ends. The house was sold and he had bought an apartment nearer work, not far from the one Andrea's father had given her.

She thought it was only right that she should say goodbye to him but he meant nothing to her now and was merely a vague reflection of a life lived long ago.

They arranged to meet in the place which had featured so much in her life, the one where she had waited for Black, the one where she had renewed her acquaintance with Ed. She didn't know why she had chosen this place. Maybe to check her own power to visit the past.

She remembered how much older he had looked as he came to towards her; pale and vulnerable and how his voice was stiff and stilted as he spoke.

'Hello, Rachel. I never expected to see you again!' he said sarcastically. She shrugged her shoulders and he continued. 'I suppose you'll be going to the States soon?' he asked, not because he wanted to but because he felt he had to. She nodded. 'It's probably for the best,' he said coldly as he stirred the coffee round in his cup and looked at her accusingly. She put the vision of their meeting out of her head and returned to the present.

'How is your sister?' Brett asked. 'Is she still seeing that guy she met at school?'

Rachel laughed.

'Yes, she's known him for a very long time. I think he's good for her. I won't worry about her so much now that she's in a good relationship. Leonie's very strong. She's a survivor.'

'What about Jeff?'

Rachel's expression changed.

'He was never the same old Jeff again. He never got over the humiliation of being used by that woman and he couldn't come to terms with the break-up of his marriage to Leonie. He lives alone in the cottage which they decided not to sell so that he could use it. He still sees the kids at weekends but he's a broken man, almost a recluse.' She stopped and drained her glass. 'I know Black lost his life which was an obvious tragedy but Jeff has lost his in a way.'

'All because of Andrea Winbech!' Brett sniffed.

'Exactly! She's got a lot to answer for.'

'Well,' said Ed, 'no doubt she'll pay for it now! She's going away for at least ten years!'

'It doesn't seem enough,' Brett said. 'I mean, she's taken a life and she'll only be in her thirties when she gets released.'

'Yes,' said Ed as he refilled their glasses. 'It's damned unfair.'

In her cell, Andrea examined the little stone as it lay in the palm of her hand—cool, smooth and sharp. She looked around for a suitable space, somewhere she could always see it so that she would never forget. Satisfied that she had found the perfect place, she held the stone between her fingers and started scratching into the surface of the wall while muttering quietly, 'It's all your fault! You took him from me! All your fault!'

She carved each initial carefully in large capital letters, eating deeply into the hard surface. R…A…C…H…E…L.

Her heart was full of hatred. When it was finished, she stood back to admire her work.

'I'll get you back someday, bitch!'

A malicious grin stretched over her face. She felt satisfied and made a resolution never to overlook the hatred she had for Rachel Mason. She would see the sign every day and plan her vengeance on release.

Later, she turned to the barred window and looked towards the vast blue sky where she caught the reflection of a silver bird intent on escape. Climbing. Soaring. Higher and higher it rose in the infinite blue expanse. Her eyes watched it move faster and faster across the sky and she longed to be on it, making her way to freedom. She did not know that on the plane, Rachel was flying to a new life with Ed by her side. Andrea Winbech could only look from her cell window and, in her bitterness, vow revenge.

The yellow field changes with the seasons. It is wintering now. Brown furrows left by the plough are frost-capped and the view is silent. Some mornings, the mist lifts and a low sun rolls in, bleaching the winter landscape. Stories are written over its surface through the decades. They blossom for a time then disappear and others take their place in a never-ending cycle.

Ingram Content Group UK Ltd.
Milton Keynes UK
UKHW021515220623
423876UK00009B/152

9 781035 813797